Fireweed

Seasons of Want and Plenty, Volume 1

Kris Farmen

Published by Blazo House, 2022.

This is a work of fiction. Similarities to real people, places, or events are entirely coincidental.

FIREWEED

First edition. December 7, 2022.

ISBN: 979-8215151990

Written by Kris Farmen.

For my girls, Jaclyn and Naia.

Another dark night has come over me.
We may never be able to return home.
But do your best in life.
That is what I do.
—Qadanalchen (Dena'ina Athabascan)

Prologue

In the spring of 1843, twenty-year-old Ivan Semyonvich Lukin carried a severed head eastward across the Bering Sea to Fort St. Michael on the coast of Russian America. It formerly belonged to a Han Chinese bureaucrat who had been swindling Lukin's employer, the Russian America Company. Packed in salt and burlap inside a basket woven of split willow wands, it rode in the bow of the open walrus-skin boat. The vessel's Malimiut captain insisted it stay as far away as possible as they drove under sail back to North America.

Lukin was not the one who chopped the head off; he was merely a courier sent over the Bering Strait the previous summer by the colony's governor. He'd been given a passport and a letter of introduction sealed with green wax, the color that signified a diplomatic envoy who was not to be harmed. The governor, Tebenkov by name, had been loath to send an ethnic Russian who would likely abscond as soon as he touched his feet to the shores of Asia. But Lukin was what was known in the colony as a Creole, a mixed-blood of Russian and Native extraction, like his father before him. His roots were in the Americas, and he would undoubtedly want to come home.

Tebenkov's calculation proved a wise one. When he returned the next year on his annual inspection tour of the colony, he was immediately satisfied when Lukin came into the boathouse at his summoning and presented the basket, setting it atop a few planks laid over a pair of sawhorses as a makeshift table.

Tebenkov prized open the friction-fit lid, then folded away the burlap. Bits of rock salt skittered across the rough boards as he grasped the braided queue and lifted the gruesome thing from its swaddlings. "So this is the one," he said to the lifeless face. The lips had sagged away from the yellowed teeth.

Lukin had never considered himself weak of stomach but he had to wrestle with a sudden queasiness that threatened to overtake him. It was hard not to think of the fresh caribou head he'd seen that morning with a Malimiut lady peeling the skin off. The naked eyeballs seemed to roll in his direction as he'd walked past. Across the table, standing behind Tebenkov was Yosif Denisov, a Creole from the Gulf of Kenay. He and Lukin had known each other since they were students in New Archangel. His eyes met Lukin's for a moment and he lifted his brows ever so slightly.

"And you witnessed the execution?" Tebenkov asked. He wore a monocle screwed into his eye and held to his navy uniform by means of a silken cord.

"I did." Lukin was just off the boat and had been looking forward to being finally rid of the damnable head. Now that he'd made the delivery it was all he could do to keep from edging toward the door. He'd been gone for a year and all he really wanted was to have a drink of rum with Denisov and the boys, and to see the rest of his family and friends who'd gathered from the far reaches of the St. Michael District for the inspection.

"Well done, Gospodin Lukin." The governor set the head back into its nest, then reached into his uniform coat and withdrew a leather wallet. From this he pulled a wad of paper scrip. He wet a thumbtip and peeled off several notes and extended them to Lukin. "Prize money for your outstanding service to the Company. Over and above your salary."

"Thank you, Your Excellency." Lukin took the money. It was large denominations, though what you could buy at the Company store at the far end of the world was, to say the least, a bit limited. He stuffed it into his vest pocket.

"I have heard nothing but praise for you," Tebenkov said, taking out his monocle and peering down his nose at Lukin. "I have no doubt that you will go far in our American enterprise."

"Thank you, sir."

Denisov had been staring at the head and the long tail of hair piled like a lump of rope. The open workshop doors let in a broad rectangle of sunlight that faded to the dark corners of the large log building. Quite suddenly Denisov's eyes bugged out. He clamped a hand to his mouth and bolted for the outside.

Tebenkov turned his head to watch as Denisov disappeared around the corner. There was the sound of retching, the green and purple of the fireweed and lupines all around. He looked back at Lukin. "I should think you will be the natural choice to replace your father at Fort Kolmakov when he retires."

"Perhaps God will so favor me."

1

FINDING BLUE — NO ONE ABOUT — ASSIGNMENT — SHAME AND HOPE — SOMEONE'S FUTURE — A BLESSING — KURILA — UPSTREAM — NO SUCH THING AS A SECRET — THE WHOLE WORLD — SUBTERFUGE — HIS MOTHER — IT CARRIES LIGHTER IN THE HEAD — PICKING FRUIT — LARGE MAN'S GIFT

A tiny piece of sky had fallen to Earth. Lukin closed the plank door behind him and carefully closed the latch so as to not waken his wife and their four-year-old son. It was maybe five in the morning and all around him Fort Nulato on the River Kwifpak still slumbered. He bent down and plucked the blue bead from its casement of packed dirt inside the palisade of spruce logs. The soil clung to it and he rubbed his thumb over the surface to let the color shine. It was style of bead he'd not seen for many years, one the Company had formerly imported from glassmakers in Venice before switching to a cheaper style sourced in China. There was no telling how long ago it had been dropped and lain there in the mud and snow.

The world was filled with May birdsong. Sticks cracked down by the riverbank; someone was building a fire for morning tea. Lukin stuck the bead in his jacket pocket then picked up his pack and his musket and walked out the gate and down to the boats in the grainy subarctic gloaming. As he approached, the figure moving about the fire formed itself into Anatoli Rudinov. He had set a kettle atop the blaze with a small pot simmering off to the side and was pottering around while it hissed, going over the boats and the rigging. Called bidaras in the colony, they were copies of the Malimiut boats on the Bering Sea with a shell of walrus hide stretched drum-tight over a wooden frame. They'd been pulled down to the beach on wooden rollers from winter storage and put in order just two days prior when the ice broke.

"Good morning, Captain," Rudinov said. He was older than Lukin, probably somewhere beyond fifty. Twenty-four years ago he'd been part of the original crew that built Fort Nulato to open up the fur trade to the colony's interior.

"Good morning. You seem to be the only one who's ready to row."

Rudinov chuckled, offering no other affirmation. "I think the water is up, if you'd like some tea."

"Yes, if you please." Lukin set his gear in the stern of his boat and fished out his tin cup. Rudinov lifted away the kettle with a stick through its bail, then the pot which held a thick concentrate of simmered tea leaves. He poured a dram of the concentrate into each of their cups, then topped it up with boiling water from the kettle. Each man added sugar to his taste. They climbed into Lukin's boat and sat on a seat and drank in silence for several minutes, watching the broad river slide past. Not even the fort dogs were barking.

"You've been to Nuklukayet before?" Lukin asked after a while.

"Many times. All the Dinneh tribes of the Interior gather there in the summer. It's where I met my wife."

Lukin was aware that Rudinov's Dinneh wife had perished some years earlier. They had a daughter, Sonia, who had been born with a simple mind and a harelip. "The river that joins the Kiwfpak there," he said.

"The Tananah."

"Yes. Nobody's ever been up it?"

"Not that I know of." Rudinov sipped at his tea.

Lukin pondered Iriana and Ilya, asleep in their beds in the tiny cabin back inside the fort. It was a fur trader's lot in life to be gone from his family for extended periods of time, and it never got any easier. He yawned, rubbed his face. He'd been awake most of the night, kept up by a mosquito and his own thoughts. It was rare these days that he slept more than an hour or two at night.

"Captain," said Rudinov.

"Mm."

"Is it true that you're going further upriver after we leave Nuklukayet?"

Lukin thought for a long moment before replying, wondering which rumors the gossip mill had hardened into fact. This rumor was true, but he'd been directed to keep his mission a secret.

"The Company is considering building a new fort up at Nuklukayet to push the trade up the Tananah and to evict the British from the Kwifpak River." This, he knew, was nothing that wasn't already circulating among Nulato's wagging tongues. "Governor Furuhjelm wants me to have a look around. Scout for timber and game, that sort of thing."

"The Hudson Bay Company has been on our ground for a good fifteen years." Rudinov gestured vaguely upriver with his cup. "They were siphoning off our furs from the upriver Indians back when I worked for Deryabin and we built this fort."

"Vasili Deryabin never had much success driving them out, as I recall," Lukin said. Everyone knew that the 141st meridian separated Russian America from what the British called Rupert's Land to the east. The Company's management, and the Czar himself, knew the Hudson Bay men were operating in violation of the international treaty that proclaimed this boundary.

"We didn't have the force of arms to challenge them." Rudinov sipped his tea. "And they controlled the Quarrelers."

Lukin pursed his lips, thinking of Maksim Vakrameev's face as he'd laid out the mission they were sending him on. He was the Company manager for the St. Michael District—bidarshik in the colonial lingo—and his domain included all the Bering Sea and the River Kwifpak, at least on paper.

"We want you to go upriver and spy on the Hudson Bay fort," he'd said over his desk in his office at St. Michael. The governor, a Finlander, sat off to the side in a chair made from staves of a broken barrel. Lukin had opened his mouth to respond, but Furuhjelm held up his hand and said they had him in mind for the job of bidarshik for the new fort at Nuklukayet. There was no such thing as a glass window north of New Archangel, and the amber light through the panes of oiled sealskin made the office look like an image printed on parchment as Furuhjelm laid a leather sack of coin on the desk in front of Lukin.

"Five hundred rubles in gold," he said, leaning back into his chair and lacing his fingers over his stomach in the posture of a man who has just finished a fine meal. "And five hundred more when you return with whatever intelligence you can gather."

Lukin had reached out for the sack and rested it in his lap. He opened it and pulled out a coin. It was a five-ruble piece, struck in gold with the image of Czar Aleksander II. Nicks in the metal showed where previous owners had bit into it to test the gold's purity. Coin of any kind was a rare thing in Russian America; Lukin's salary was still paid in the colonial paper scrip. Gold was rarer still. Once on the upper forks of the River Kuskokwim, a hunter from the Koltsan people had showed Lukin a handful of musketballs he'd cast from gold nuggets washed from the river in a birchbark pan. When Lukin had asked the man why he'd chosen this particular material he just shrugged and said he'd run out of lead. The gold, he claimed, didn't fly as true, but with careful aim would bring down a moose or a mountain sheep. Beyond that the hunter had placed no value whatsoever on the gleaming yellow metal.

Vakrameev had been watching Lukin with a level gaze over the top of his desk. Behind him on the wall were tacked a series of maps and nautical charts, mostly of Spanish and British imprint. The labels and names in their indecipherable Latin script were struck out with a single line of ink. Cyrillic translations were penned above in a small, neat hand.

"They tell me," said the governor, "that you were demoted to the status of common laborer following the unpleasantness at Fort Kolmakov."

Lukin had been made to stand in formation with the district's working men for the governor's inspection the day before. All the whispers about him as the Romanov colors flapped in the stiff wind that raced across the treeless Bering Sea coast. The prince of the Creoles, fallen to Earth. That he just couldn't measure up to his father, the renowned trader Semyon Lukin.

Lukin cleared his throat. "The Company very graciously allowed me to keep my management-level salary."

"I would say," Vakrameev began as Lukin closed up the sack, "that this prospect is your opportunity to redeem yourself to the Company."

"To repair your good name," Furuhjelm added. Once again Lukin was made to taste the shame of his demotion. There seemed to be no end to the people who wanted to remind him of it.

* * *

"Did you bring the cards?" Lukin asked Rudinov. The swallows were out for the morning, zooming to and fro above their heads as they chased mosquitoes above the fort's palisade.

"I did."

"Any chance I could get a reading?"

"I suppose." Rudinov set his cup on the seat next to him and fished around in his packsack until he withdrew a deck of tarot cards in a sliding wooden box. Long ago in a former life he'd been a circus performer, and if prompted with enough rum could tell stories about riding elephants, boxing matches with kangaroos, and doing high-wire acts in Prague, Trieste, Vienna, and Moscow.

"Cruciform?" he said as he shuffled.

"Yes."

"Think of a question you'd like an answer to."

"There are so many."

"Try to focus on just one."

Will I ever get my life back seemed to be the only one Lukin could muster. It was no less heartfelt for being so inane.

Rudinov rapped the deck endwise on the seat and spread the cards out in a line between them. Lukin drew five at random and handed them over. Rudinov gathered up the deck and set it aside and turned the first card. "The Moon."

Lukin had a longstanding relationship with the moon. "What does that mean?" He glanced up at the horizon to see if she was watching them.

"There's this path down the middle." Rudinov pointed at the colored woodcut image stamped on the card. "The towers and the land on either side mirror one another. It's hard to tell good from evil, right from wrong. You're starting out in the dark of night taking a path you are unsure of."

"That is most certainly true."

"But the moon's light brings clarity."

"Clarity," he said. That was one thing you could call it.

Rudinov turned the next card. "Ten of Wands. You see the man carrying that bundle of firewood?"

"Yes."

"He's carrying this heavy load on his back, and he's almost home."

"But the card is upside down," Lukin said, pointing.

"That means you won't get to set your burden down any time soon."

Lukin grunted. He'd never really understood what it was he searched for in a tarot reading. Ever since getting fired from Fort Kolmakov the cards seemed as devoid of meaning as everyday life.

"Shall I go on?"

"Please."

Rudinov turned the following card and set it down on the seat with an audible slap. "Temperence."

The corner of Lukin's mouth turned up. "I was afraid I'd get that one."

"It's also reversed for you. That means you don't have a clear idea of what you're trying to accomplish in your life."

Lukin tried to come up with some smart comment but could find nothing through the haze of sleeplessness. His eyes felt like they were full of sawdust. The tea had helped, but only a little. Rudinov watched him.

"Go on."

"Generally this card means you should focus your energy on working in harmony with the people around you."

"You mean my boat crew?"

Rudinov shrugged. "You asked for a reading, Captain. I just speak what's in the cards."

"Fair enough. Next, please."

"Four of Swords," Rudinov said, laying the card down below the Moon to begin making the shape of the cross.

Lukin studied the image of the knight laying prone with three swords dangling over him and a fourth beneath his bed. He'd seen the other cards before in previous readings, but not this one. "What does this mean?"

"The time has come to withdraw from battle for a while and let your wounds heal. You've faced one crisis after another, and it's time to take a break. Let your mind rest."

Fort Kolmakov, thought Lukin. *Everybody always wants to talk about Fort Kolmakov.* The trading fort had been founded by his father, and upon his father's death he'd been promoted to bidarshik. Then came the famine. The mutiny. The leaving and the inquest. The shame of realizing that while he knew the fur trade inside and out, he just wasn't management material. Now the only home he'd known since he was thirteen was lost to him.

Rudinov's face remained impassive.

"Last card," Lukin said.

He noted the scrim of dirt under Rudinov's battered thumbnail as he turned the final card to the top of the cross. "The Queen of Cups."

Lukin waited for the explanation.

Rudinov tapped a finger upon the image. "This means there's a lady coming into your life. One who leads with her heart instead of her head. The suit of cups stands for water, so my guess is you'll meet her by a river or the sea."

"I am married, you know."

"Tarot cards don't lie."

Lukin frowned at the queen sitting on her throne at the edge of the sea, staring at the cup in her hand. There was someone he knew would be following him with the moon. But she didn't look anything like this queen. Then again, the images on the cards never did look like the taiga forests, silty rivers, and open tundra of Russian America.

"Thank you," he said and tossed the dregs of his tea into the sand. He climbed over the gunwale, then dug into his jacket pocket and withdrew a two ruble note. "That is the last reading I will ask you for."

"I've heard that before."

"I'm a man of my word. Whatever anyone else may tell you."

Rudinov pocketed the money without further comment and Lukin poured them another cup of tea. They went back to watching the river.

* * *

Everyone at Nulato—indentured Russians, the local Denakeh and Deghitan people, and Creoles of all ages—gathered to farewell the boats on their departure to Nuklukayet. Lukin's bidara was one of three making the annual trip. For several years the Company had been sending a flotilla upriver to the trading fair, largely in response to the incursions of the Hudson Bay Company. Each vessel carried several hundred pounds of merchandise for the Dinneh Indians upriver: copper kettles, steel axes and knives, guns, blankets and stroud cloth, and vermilion for red paint, as well as kegs of highly-prized seal oil and coils of unbreakable rope made from walrus hide. The Dinneh had always been demanding customers and had lately become even more so now that they had the option of selling their fur catch to the British out of Fort Youcon. British goods, they claimed, were far superior to what the Company offered, though Lukin assumed this was at least in part an attempt to play the British off against the Russians for a better deal. He would have done the same had he been in their position.

The parish priest, Father Netsvetov, could not be at Nulato to bless the departure; his flock was scattered over a thousand square miles of wilderness and he only came around once or twice each year. Lukin, however, had been trained in New Archangel as a song-leader for the church, and was asked by the people to stand in for him.

He stood before the assembled crowd and opened his worn prayer book. He caught his wife looking at him as she stood at the front holding four-year-old Ilya's hand. She looked away, down at the ground, then the river, then at Ilya's hair. Anywhere but at her husband. She'd barely smiled at him since their reassignment to the St. Michael District.

There was nothing to do for the moment but recite the prayer. Lukin cleared his throat and the crowd bowed their heads as he chanted the liturgy in Slavonic for their task to be completed. Robins and thrushes filled the air; somewhere nearby a raven's wings whistled in the wind. The sled dogs, sitting idle this time of year, barked and yowled. When he'd finished the first prayer he moved to another for God's protection for those heading into the unknown. He'd recited these incantations so many times he barely needed the book, but the book and the prayer were one and the same, so he always flipped to the appropriate page and followed along with his fingertip as he sang.

Iriana had always had the sinful habit of looking up during prayer. She was by birth an Ikogmiut from the lower Kwifpak, ancient enemies of the Interior Dinneh tribes, but she had lived most of her life in their country. Back when she'd converted to Christianity as a young woman, she'd voiced to him the notion that the whispering of running water was what she thought the voice of God sounded like, and this had never really left Lukin's mind. It seemed as accurate a notion as any, since God appeared to have deserted them. Prayers lately had acquired a hollow sound in his mind. They were muscle memory and voice, nothing more than paper cutouts of a devotion he no longer felt. But rivers. Rivers and the sound they made were always there.

When the makeshift service was completed, Lukin crossed himself again and kissed his fingertips in deference to the sacred. Rote memory and nothing more, like he was living underwater. The single men assigned to the boats climbed over the gunwales and moved to their places. The married men took a last moment to embrace their families.

"Travel with God," Iriana said as he hugged her.

"My heart always stays with you two." Lukin buried his fingertips in the hair at the base of her neck as he nuzzled her. She'd been bothered with lice lately, but then half the people at the fort had them at any given time so it wasn't something worth complaining about. But there would be no canoe picnics, no watching birds or building stick forts with Ilya. No pretending to be a fish swimming on dry land and making them both cut up with laughter. No love-making with Iriana late at night or out in the forest. Not that there had been very much of that in the last year.

He sighed, hunkering down so he was at eye level with his son. "Do you see that fireweed over there?"

"Yes."

The tiny shoots had pushed up through the thatch of last year's dead grass on the bank. "I will be coming home when that fireweed tops out with its first blooms. It's your job to be the man of the house while I'm away." The boy's dark eyes were serious like pools of night. "Your number one task is to behave yourself and help your mother any way you can."

"Papa, when is Anastasia coming home?"

Lukin pressed his lips together. "We've talked about this already." She was Ilya's half-sister, Lukin's daughter from his first marriage.

"I miss her."

"I know," he said, though he was pretty certain the lad barely remembered her. "But she's away at school in New Archangel. She won't be home for a few years."

Ilya's mouth turned down, then brightened. "When you come back I'll have the blanket house ready."

This was a game they often played where they would sit on the floor and throw a blanket over themselves for no purpose other than to sit together. Ilya would kneel on Lukin's lap and play with his beard and knead his small palms into his father's cheeks as he studied his eyes.

Lukin smiled. "Now can you do those things I told you?"

"Yes, Papa."

"All right." He opened his arms. "Come here, lad." The boy's breath was warm against his chest in the open collar of his shirt, taking his mind back to when he'd held him as an infant. He would instantly start fussing if you didn't hold him so he was facing out and could watch the world. Time passed so fast and there was ultimately not much you could do but worry about them. His only other son, Dmitri, had died in his bed at the age of five many years before back on the Kuskokwim, and his secret fear was that God had designs to take Ilya from him as well.

He stood and rumpled Ilya's mop of stiff hair, which his mother insisted they keep cut short in the Russian fashion, then he looked over at Iriana. "Stay safe, my love," he said in Malimiut.

She nodded and wouldn't look at him.

Sergei Metrikov, the Nulato bidarshik, passed around tin cups with a finger of Hawaiian rum in them. Lukin took the cup that was pressed into his hand by Ivan Denisov, who by now had worked his way up to second in charge at Nulato. Metrikov had put him in command of the flotilla because he himself was getting too old to go and he flatly refused to have Lukin in charge. The boss was a former soldier, and had said of Lukin, or so he heard, that he had no use for a man who loses a fight. The implication was that he was only allowing Lukin to go upriver because he had been commanded to do so by his own superiors.

"I guess I only rate the cheap stuff," Lukin whispered, peering into the cup. Vodka from St. Petersburg was far too expensive to waste on colonials so the Company imported rum from the Pacific kingdom at rock-bottom prices. About all you could say for it was that it got the job done.

Denisov smirked. "My friend, everyone here only deserves cheap rum in Metrikov's eyes."

The men in the boat and those still on shore waited as Metrikov spoke his toast. "Gentlemen of the Russian America Company, we have prayed to God for your safe passage. And now we pray to the spirits." He lifted his cup into the air. "I wish you a safe journey, profitable commerce, and a speedy return. To your health!"

They drank and the cups were passed back to be returned to the store inventory. Denisov clapped Lukin on the shoulder and moved down the beach to his boat. Next to him the third boat's captain, a Creole named Sava Golinov was already in the stern. He was also from the Gulf of Kenay and his blood was a mix of virtually every ethnic group to be found in the colony—Aleut, Kolosh, Russian, and Dinneh. And maybe, Lukin had often reckoned since they'd all been at school together, some Siberian Tungus or Chukchi thrown in for good measure.

Lukin was just making ready to climb into his boat when a Dinneh youth dressed in Russian clothes sauntered up with his duffel slung over his shoulder. Long black hair spilled down his back.

"Kurila," Lukin said.

"The bidarshik said I am to row with your crew."

Lukin squinted at him. "How old are you? Twelve?"

"Thirteen." The lad was clearly over the moon at the prospect of the trip.

"Thirteen."

Kurila was Denakeh by birth, these being the Dinneh people of the lower Kwifpak and the River Koyukuk. He'd been orphaned at the age of three when his parents were slain in an attack on Fort Nulato back in 1851. He was, however, even at his young age, reputed to be one of the finest marksmen at the fort, and one of the top hunters.

"This isn't child's play," Lukin said. "I will expect you to row like a man."

Kurila's posture stiffened. "I can pull an oar as good as anyone."

The attack on Nulato been led by a Denakeh chief named Larion, who, Lukin was aware, knew of Kurila and would likely be at Nuklukayet. He glanced again at Metrikov. The bidarshik's word was law, so it wasn't as if he had any say in the matter anyway. "Come aboard, then."

Kurila's smile, as always, was contagious, reminding Lukin not a little of when he'd been that age and was finally allowed to go up the Kuskokwim with his father to the country of the Koltsan people, the warlike Dinneh hunters who lived in the mountains around forks of the river.

"Boatmen," Denisov called out. "Let's get moving!"

"I love you," Lukin called out to his wife and son, lifting a hand.

Ilya waved at him but Iriana kept her hands at her sides. There was nothing to be done about that now.

Lukin climbed into the stern and his crew—Kurila and Rudinov, plus four other men whose names he was still learning—hoisted the bow of the boat and pushed it into the river. Lukin's men gave the vessel a final push, then hopped over the bow with a splash.

"I've missed wet feet," Rudinov said as he lifted his oar and set it in the lock. His moccasins sluiced water as he moved. Lukin as captain got the privilege of keeping his feet dry, at least for the moment. That was bound to go out the window before the day was done. There was just no good way to keep your feet dry when you were working around boats.

The other crews had their oars in play. Denisov's boat was already drawing upriver against the current, with Sava's crew holding steady against the flow while they picked up speed. You could hear Sava shouting out encouragement to them, exhorting them to put their backs into it and not make an embarrassing show of things right in front of the fort and their families. Eventually their boat began making headway.

"Alright, boys," Lukin said, "let's tuck in right behind Sava."

Like a lot of the local workmen rowing his boat, Lukin wore Dinneh-style trousers made of soft caribou leather with the moccasins sewn onto each leg to make a single one-piece garment. Over these it had long been his habit to wear a second pair of moccasins tied around his calves with leather cord. His vest was of Spanish cut, imported from California; the shirt beneath was of the old Russian style with no cuffs or collar and the neck opening off to the side. He kept the tail belted around his waist in the Russian fashion. His peajacket was getting a bit threadbare; earlier that spring Iriana had sewn leather patches onto the elbows so he could get another year's wear out of it.

Standing in the stern, Lukin paused to fold and knot a kerchief around his head as Sava and Denisov's crews bent to their oars. Everyone was rusty from not rowing all winter and their strokes were not well-timed.

Lukin's own crew wasn't doing any better, but he preferred not to yell at his men unless he really had to. "All right boys," he said, "let's work at keeping your oars in better time. We all know the boat moves better when you all pull as one." He coughed, spat a wad of phlegm over the side. "It's a long way to the fair at Nuklukayet, so don't wear yourselves out in the first hour."

Kurila glanced at him as he reefed back on his oar, but the other men—convicts, most of them—kept their eyes fixed over the stern into empty space somewhere over the river. Lukin hoped he wouldn't have to flog any of them. Corporal punishment had just been made illegal in the colony, but the reach of the Czar's law evaporated beyond the first bend upriver from Nulato.

* * *

The first rule of camping along the Kwifpak was to find a wide exposed gravel bar where there would be a breeze to keep away the mosquitoes. The first night they stopped somewhere around six o'clock by Denisov's reckoning. Nobody had a timepiece and Ursa Major was nowhere to be seen in the eternal summer daylight, but Denisov was known for his ability to keep time by his internal clock when there was neither stars nor sun to go by.

This was the first time Lukin, Denisov, and Sava Golinov had been all three together since for almost ten years. They drafted young Kurila as their camp boy, though everyone worked to gather firewood and pitch the sailcloth lean-tos and mosquito nets they would sleep under. Kurila didn't take much convincing; he was possessed of the boundless rubber-limbed energy of youth and recognized that it was far more pleasant to camp with the officers than with the crew.

He got their fire going with flint and steel, then expertly set the kettle atop the blazing sticks. The boat captains relaxed with their backs against their blanket rolls and packs, loading their pipes with Chinese tobacco. They passed around a flaming brand from the fire to light up. Each carried phosphorus matches, but these were not always available and the prevailing wisdom was that it was best to save them for when they were truly needed and wouldn't be instantly snuffed out by the wind.

Sava pulled his pipestem from his mouth and blew a gentle cloud of smoke. "So is it true that you're headed upriver after Nuklukayet to spy on the British?"

"I see there's no such thing as a secret up here," Lukin said. He'd not spoken a word of the plan, so he could only surmise that Metrikov or someone higher up had let it slip.

"I was glad to hear they're giving you another chance," Denisov said. "You got a raw deal over Fort Kolmakov."

Lukin smoked without comment. Both these friends understood way down in their marrow the difficulties he'd faced, being three-quarters Native and trying to manage a staff of white men who considered him their racial inferior.

"It's true," he said. "They want me to go up to that Hudson Bay fort and have a look around." He paused, looking into the fire. "Fort Youcon, they call it."

"Youcon?" said Sava.

"That's what the British call the Kwifpak," Lukin said. "Or so I'm told."

"How do you aim to proceed?" Denisov asked. Sava watched from across the fire as Kurila dumped a handful of tea into a small pot and set it to simmer. He laid more wood on the fire then put a larger copper pot atop it with more water for soup. From a few rods away, the boatmen let out a roar of laughter over something or other.

Sava lifted one buttock and let out a commendably loud fart. "That's what I have to say about that," he said, tipping his head to the crew.

His fellow captains smirked.

Kurila sat back on his knees, leaning away from the smoke. "Where is Fort Youcon?"

"Nobody really knows," Denisov said.

"I have a map of the whole world."

"A map?" said Lukin.

Kurila bent over to his kit bag and rummaged inside. After a moment he withdrew a rectangle of battered paper. He moved over so he was next to Lukin and unfolded it. The cartouche in the lower right corner bore the date of 1849. The paper was frayed at the folds with holes in several of the joints. Dark rings showed where teacups had been set atop it and there was a large translucent grease stain to the southwest of Ceylon.

"Where did you get that?" Denisov asked.

"Maksim Vakrameev gave it to me when he was at Nulato in February."

Lukin pointed at the Americas, both North and South. "Do you know where Russian America is?" He was aware the lad had never been to school and couldn't read.

Kurila screwed his mouth up, thinking hard.

"It's here," Lukin pointed his index finger down to the paper. Russian America was colored a pale blue, the same as all the Russian Empire. Queen Victoria's North American holdings including Rupert's Land were shown in red. The United States of America were shown in yellow, as were China, France, Morocco, and the Argentine Republic. Russia's sole American colony was a small-looking place when laid against the immensity of the entire world, and that view didn't quite square up with how far he had to travel on his assignment. It was at least a Russian map, lettered in Cyrillic. Lukin traced the outline of the colony, really the entire northwest lobe of the continent, with his fingertip. He pointed to a tiny label on the Bering Sea coast that read, *St. Michael.* "This dot here is Fort St. Michael."

"Where is Nulato?" Kurila peered around the side of Lukin's finger.

Lukin moved the finger up the squiggly line that represented the River Kwifpak. "It isn't shown on this map, but this blue line is the river."

Kurila seemed fascinated almost beyond words. "The Kwifpak there?" He hooked a thumb toward the water, a scant ten fathoms away from where they sat.

"The very same. Do you see this line here?"

"The long straight one?"

"Yes. That's the 141st meridian. It scores the boundary between the Russian Empire and the British Empire. We don't know precisely where Fort Youcon is, but we're pretty sure it's on the Russian side of the line. The Hudson Bay Company built it fifteen years ago in violation of a treaty between the Czar and Queen Victoria. And they've been sending boats down to Nuklukayet every summer to steal even more furs from us."

Kurila stared at the map, plainly captivated by the notion that the river they were camped on could be traced on a piece of paper. The kid had a good heart but was as unworldly as they come. Lukin thought it an abject shame that he had not been sent to school.

"So," said Denisov.

Lukin lifted his eyebrows.

"How are you going to get into that British fort?"

"I haven't decided. I mean, it's hard to make a plan until I get a look at it and see what I'm dealing with."

"What about just walking up to the gate and telling the Canadians you're a deserter from the Russian America Company?" Sava asked. He had a knack for making suggestions that were about fifty-one percent serious or the same percent facetious, but you really had to know him well to know which was which.

"Well, for one thing, I don't speak any English."

"I thought Canadians spoke French," said Sava. Kurila abandoned his map to pour out the tea. He handed Sava a cup with sugar and Sava poured hot water from the kettle to top it up.

"I don't speak French either."

"In the hands of a lesser man, that might be a problem," Sava said.

Lukin watched the local swallows as they swooped and dove from a high bluff just upstream. His attention was only drawn away when Denisov passed him the sugar.

Kurila looked up with him. "Is it true they eat mosquitoes?"

"It is," Lukin said, grateful for the change of subject. "Bats eat them too."

"And dragonflies. That's what Metrikov says, anyway."

God only knew why the boy thought so highly of the Nulato bidarshik. The man rarely had a kind word for him, or anybody for that matter. He seemed to resent being saddled with the lad's care, which would explain his eagerness to get him out on a rowing crew as soon as he could. But then Lukin had observed more than once that the children of abusive fathers, or father figures, often toiled in vain to please them. He himself had been blessed with a kind and loving father, and was all too aware of the fact that many children in this world weren't so fortunate. Denisov's father, from what Lukin had gathered over the years, had been little more than a drunken bully.

"Your soup water's up," Denisov said to Kurila, gesturing with his cup.

Kurila got down on one knee and opened a sack of dried caribou meat. This he crumbled into the simmering water in generous measure, then he dug into their waterproof sack of rusks made from the standard black bread baked at all Russian forts. He smashed it up with the butt of an axe and dumped it into the pot with a little salt.

"Seriously, though," Denisov said. "How do you plan to get inside the fort?"

"I'll see about buying a suit of Dinneh clothes at Nuklukayet. Figured I'd slip in disguised as a Quarreler."

"What's a Quarreler?" Kurila asked, looking up.

"They're the people who live upriver around the British fort."

"You don't speak their language either." Denisov's eyes moved up as a swallow darted low over their fire then disappeared.

"True," said Lukin. "But I'm pretty good with languages."

* * *

When he was six years old, Lukin's mother received instructions in a dream that she should take her son to visit his grandparents. They were at the time still wintering at Fort Aleksander on the lower reaches of the Nushagak River. Fort Kolmakov had yet to be built. His father Semyon Lukin, then a young man in his prime, had been leading trading expeditions every year up the Nushagak, then over the arduous portage to the headwaters of the Hohlitna River, and then down to the Kuskokwim, a vast river that was thought to drain at least a third of the colony. Ivan had been going on these journeys since he could remember. They would get down to the mouth of the Hohlitna to a cabin Semyon and his men had built some years before; the local Deghitan and Kenaytze people would congregate to sell furs there, much like at Nuklukayet. Semyon had met and married Lukin's Deghitan mother on one of these early trips.

It must have been 1829 or 1830. The market for beaver pelts was still booming, and they had just made it to the trading outpost when the next morning his mother told Semyon that she intended to go upriver to see her parents and family.

"I want our son to see his country so he can know the old stories," he recalled her saying around their fire outside the house.

Semyon, himself a colony-born Creole with roots on Kodiak Island, had frowned into his tea. "That's a long trip. The boy is young."

"We drag them upriver and over the portage every year," she countered. "A few more days of travel won't hurt him."

They left later that day in a birchbark canoe, just the two of them. Lukin's mother was always tearful at departures but she sat in the stern of the canoe and he in the bow, and every time he twisted around to look at her she told him to face the front so the boat wouldn't tip over.

They paddled when they could, keeping close to shore where the swirling back eddies of the river made for easier going. When they couldn't paddle they got out and tracked the canoe upstream along footpaths that paralleled the river for that very purpose. Their route took them up the Kuskokwim, then up a slackwater slough on the north side, then into another slough. At some point they turned up a smallish tributary, but young Lukin was thoroughly lost by this point. When he got scared about this, his mother held him close and smiled at him and reminded him that she'd grown up here and knew exactly where they were.

One afternoon the canoe's birchbark shell was torn open by an underwater snag and started taking on water. They pulled into shore and his mother took their axe and led him into a stand of birch trees. Mosquitoes flew in a cloud all around them, but she smeared a mixture of fish oil and Russian birch tar all over their skin, which made things more tolerable.

"You want to help me peel a birch tree?" she asked.

"Alright."

She drove the axe head into a fallen log nearby, then took out her knife and cut a long slit down the length of the trunk, then scribed two lines girthwise around it, about three feet apart. The vertical slit had already begun to pull apart from the release in tension as she traded the knife for the axe and started working the bit under one of the leading edges. Squinting against the bugs, she mentioned that the bark didn't peel quite as easy in high summer as in springtime, but it could still be done if you took it slow.

"What did you do before you had a steel axe?" Lukin asked her.

She smiled. "Wait here. She peered this way and that through the trees, then she walked over and cut a long alder limb, wrist-thick at its base. With a few deft strokes of the axe, then her knife, she whittled the fat end down to a wide paddle with a gently rounded edge, not unlike a wooden spatula.

"You can work this under the edge like an axe. Of course when I was young all we had was knives and axes made of stone, which took a lot longer." She held the paddle out to him. "Give it a try."

Lukin stepped up to the tree and pushed it into the junction where the rind was still stuck to the bright green underbark.

"Not so hard," his mother said. "Go easy or you'll tear it." The sheet was about halfway off the trunk and she stepped around to hold the free edge and bend it back a little to make the peeling easier. Instantly it became less work to get the paddle's edge underneath and gently pry the sheet loose.

When it finally snapped free she laid a hand on his head, saying, "Good job." She tickled his ribs, something he was getting a little too old for, but he laughed anyway. She pointed to the peeling paddle in his hand. "You don't need a lot of fancy Russian stuff to make things work in the forest. You can just make a tool like that on the spot and leave it behind when you're done." She tapped her temple with a finger. "It's a lot easier to carry it in your head than on your back."

The next morning, in the middle stretches of the tributary, she pointed the canoe into shore. "We're going to walk for a bit."

"What for, Mama?"

"I saw the first ripe blueberries. And there's a friend I want you to meet who lives hereabouts."

They had bark left over from the patching job, and she folded it into a bucket held together by spruce root stitches and a willow wand bent into a hoop to form the rim. Lukin watched as she sat cross-legged on the beach and sewed the hoop onto the rim with an awl and more split spruce roots. When the bucket was finished—a scant twenty minutes of work—they walked into the muskeg and found good picking.

"Ivan!" she said at one point.

Young Lukin stopped with a handful of blueberries and a purple rim around his lips.

"Stop eating so many. Put them in the bucket, not in your mouth!"

"Sorry." They were the very taste of summer, the only time of year there was such a thing as fresh fruit in their lives. He'd seen her pop more than a few choice berries into her own mouth.

"We're going to take them to my friend as a gift," she said. "It'll take forever to get enough if you keep eating them."

"Alright."

When the bucket was finally full she led him farther across the muskeg. Eventually the black spruce grew closer together, then there were a few birches and willows, a sure sign that drier ground was up ahead.

"Where are we going?" Lukin asked. The country didn't look like anything special.

"Rest easy, Ivan. I've been here many times."

The trees gradually formed a forest around them. Lukin had no idea where they were, but then he hadn't had any inkling for some days.

They stopped in front of an enormous birch tree and a white spruce of similar girth, both growing from the same base. Lukin peered up at this oddity, waving at the mosquitoes. One half of the amalgamated trunk was wrapped in smooth birchbark, the other in the scaly bark of the spruce. The trunk forked apart at the height of a grown man's shoulder.

His mother pulled him back a few steps, then spoke a word Lukin didn't recognize. It sounded to his ear more like aspen leaves rustling in the wind than an actual word.

Nothing happened for several heartbeats. A thrush called from deep in the woods. Mosquitoes buzzed in and out of their ears. There was the whistling of a raven's wings as it flew overhead, bound for points unknown. Then the twin trees started shaking and to Lukin's utter astonishment a circle of earth opened like the hatch on a ship's hold. An enormous hand with fingers easily as long as Lukin's entire body pushed the rootwad over onto its side, then an equally enormous head poked up from the hole. It looked about the size of their cabin back at the Hohlitna River. Young Lukin had heard tales of giants told around the winter fires, but had never expected to see such a creature in the flesh.

"Who calls?" said the large man, squinting at them.

"It's me," said his mother.

He leaned his head in their direction. From chin to forehead his face was easily as tall as Lukin's mother. He smiled. "Yinehbaa."

This was Lukin's mother's real name; at Fort Aleksander the Russians called her Ludmila.

"I have not seen you for a very long time," he said.

"I've been away. This is my son, Ivan."

"Yeevon? What manner of name is that?"

"Ee-van," she corrected. "His father is Russian."

"I don't know what a Russian is."

"They are strangers who came from the other side of the western sea."

"Are they beings of intelligence?"

"Not for the most part. But they bring nice things to sell."

The giant scrunched up his face in thought, then blinked several times in rapid succession. The notion of the sea having another side seemed slightly more than he could ken. Slowly, he climbed from his underground house, getting first one elbow onto the edge of the hole, then the other, and stepping up so that he stood before them. Lukin was barely three feet tall and the creature looked as tall as the sky itself. He stood with his head and shoulders above the forest canopy. An envious stature, Lukin thought, for it would enable him to see over the tops of the trees, all the way across the rolling hills.

The giant looked this way and that, then yawned and stretched, which had the effect of making him even taller. When he was satisfied they were alone he hunkered down in front of them. The twinned spruce and birch tree swayed to and fro as he tipped the treeroot door to his house closed.

"So long since I saw you last," he said to Lukin's mother.

"I've been away. I'm married now. Ivan's father and I spend the winters south of here." His mother paused, then said, "Have you seen anything interesting in the forest lately?"

The giant scratched his chin, thinking. "I saw three moose calves born to one mother back in the spring. I also saw a hummingbird."

"A hummingbird?" The tiny bird was known to the Deghitan, though it did not normally inhabit their lands.

"Yes. I had been sitting by the river for several days watching the fish when he came up to me and buzzed around my face." He smiled. "I think maybe she wanted to make a nest in my hair." The giant shook his head, then yawned again. "How many of these Russians are there?"

"Plenty," his mother said.

"And what do they want?"

"They come to buy furs from us. They pay with steel knives and axes, and copper cooking pots." As a grown man, Lukin would come to know that there was a lot his mother left unsaid about how the Russians did business, but at such a tender age he didn't know any different.

"What is *steel*?"

"It's like copper, but harder. It holds a better edge."

The giant seemed disturbed by this. He peered at Lukin, leaning down on one elbow so as to get his head right down next to the ground. Lukin did his best not to be scared. Slowly, the giant stretched out his pointer finger at him. Lukin, not knowing any better and refusing to be afraid, held out his own finger so that the tips touched. The bulb of the giant's finger was the size of a blown-up sealgut float. The enormous man smiled at him.

"Does your son talk?"

"Of course. He can speak both our language and Russian quite well." He heard more than a little pride coloring his mother's voice.

"Have you killed any game yet?" he asked Lukin.

Lukin's heart hammered against the inside of his ribcage. "No," he managed to say. "But we brought you some berries." He'd been lugging the large bucket for the last half mile, and it now seemed minuscule.

"I don't understand these words."

At his mother's urging, Lukin repeated the words in Deghitan.

The giant's face brightened. "You speak very well indeed," he said. "I don't know many youngsters who are so articulate as you."

"Thank you," he said in Russian. He hefted the berry bucket with both hands so the giant could grasp it. It looked like a teacup between his thumb and forefinger.

"More of those bizarre words." The giant tipped some of the berries into his palm and pushed them into his mouth. "I love blueberries more than anything, but they are so hard for me to pick with my big fingers."

"You could try eating them straight off the bush like a big animal." *Big animal* was the common way to refer to a bear.

The giant grinned. "I'm rather large too." He ate another handful of berries, apparently turning something over in his mind. He said, "Your son is clever, and good with words. I think when he is older he will speak all the languages of the country without any trouble." Gently he reached out his forefinger and patted Lukin's head. "Just listen to the trees and the birds, young man. They will tell you what people are saying."

The following year, when his mother fell through the springtime ice and drowned, Lukin would think of this very moment. The world was full of strange beings but it would be a long time before he would see another large man.

2

AQUEOUS MEMORY — MORNING ON THE RIVER — CROW AND THE MOSQUITOES — KOLOSH MOON — NOWIKAKET — KWIFPAK SALUTE — THE WIDOW — WORK OF THE SHAMAN — AWAKE — ZIA — SEEING IS BELIEVING — AN ATTACK INTERRUPTED — GOD IS UP IN HEAVEN — FLOG WELL — FAMINE AND MUTINY ON THE KUSKOKWIM — IMPRISONED TOGETHER

He woke to the crackle of Kurila building up the fire for the morning's tea. Beyond was the velvet sound of the river sliding over the rocks, the sand, the gravel on its way to the Bering Sea. Somewhere just upstream there was a sweeper tree hanging in the current and he could hear in the morning quiet water sluicing through its boughs and needles while the roots clung to the shore and to life itself with a white-knuckle grip.

His earliest memories were of moving water and since childhood he had been entranced by the sound it made and the blue sky reflected on its skin. It was a pleasure that often filled his dreams, when he managed to get some sleep, but this morning his dreams had been focused on his first wife Natalia. They had been standing at a river's edge in September. He knew the time of year because of the leathery aspen leaves floating in a dark eddy behind her. She had been half Russian and half Koltsan; the shape of her eyes was entirely Russian, with the wide mouth and dark hair of the Dinneh. In the dream she was smiling and the smile as always lit up her entire face. She was happy because he'd handed her a blue bead he'd found in his pocket, and that's when the dream fled and the world came rushing in well before he was ready to confront it.

He blinked his eyes at the river, missing her and her smile. He had long since given up wondering if it was sinful for a widower to dwell on thoughts of his deceased wife while married to another woman. Natalia had died before they had the chance to grow unhappy together, and he had to fight hard against a nascent wish that Iriana might do the same. Actually, not so much a well-formed desire as an acknowledgment that it would be a convenient escape from their crumbling marriage. He and Natalia were never really meant to be together, or so he'd believed since he proposed to Iriana. But then it was probably best to put such thoughts back in the box where they couldn't do more damage.

Lukin opened his eyes for good and drew back his blanket and peajacket over top of that. Yawning, he reached into the jacket's pocket and felt around the shapes of his flint and steel and a loose jumble of leather thong until his fingers touched the blue bead, buried in the deep inside corner.

Kurila added more wood to the flames. Lukin sighed and stretched his arms, thinking again of the giant. The pain in his left shoulder had returned. He'd noticed it back in February, but it had gradually faded away during Lent. He had no idea what he might have done to cause it. *I guess I'm getting old enough to collect aches and pains,* he realized. It was a disquieting thought with which to start the day.

"Good morning, Captain," Kurila said. The breeze had fizzled out during the night and the bugs had returned with a renewed zeal. Kurila wore a kerchief tied bandit-style over his nose and mouth to keep from inhaling them. He also followed the smoke around the campfire as much as possible. On the far side of the hearth Sava and Denisov both stirred in their blankets, rumpled forms wrapped in cocoons of wool and canvas.

"Good morning." Lukin sat up as much as he could under the mosquito bar, propping one elbow beneath him. He rubbed his eyes, then untied the side flap of the netting and rolled out into the bugs. He walked away several steps and untied his pants and released his morning urine. It was difficult to keep a steady aim for all the waving he did as the bugs crawled over him. When finished he tied a kerchief over his face as Kurila had done, then pulled his slouchy cap down low over his head.

Each boat carried a sack of gudge, a woody conk fungus harvested from the trunks of dead birch trees. Lukin went to his boat, found the sack, and withdrew several chunks. The boats were also equipped with old copper pots, each with a row of holes punched around the lower rim for air.

Over the fire, Lukin used a stick to scrape a few hot coals into the pot, then he placed several gudge chunks atop them. This done, he placed the whole thing atop the fire to get it going hot and fast. Kurila set the tea to simmer for a moment before taking it off to steep. By the time it was ready the peculiar sour-sweet gudge smoke billowed up from the censer to fill the air around them. The mosquitoes beat a hasty retreat.

"They sure hate the smell of that stuff, Kurila said, pulling the cloth down from his nose and mouth before handing Lukin a mug of tea. Sava and Denisov had wandered away for their morning piss at the water's edge.

"There's an old Dinneh story about gudge." Lukin dipped a little cold water from the camp bucket into his tea to cool it down for drinking. "That after Crow created the world the mosquitoes bothered him so much that he made gudge by pissing on a birch tree." The story was actually about Raven, the ubiquitous black bird trickster, but he'd been trained from childhood to use the name Crow in deference to the power the bird wielded over people's lives. He took a tentative sip from his cup.

"And that's why it smells the way it does?"

Lukin pointed a sly finger at him by way of answer. The other two captains hunkered by the fire for their tea. Sava's wavy hair dripped water onto his shoulders from where he'd washed his face in the silty river.

A nearby wooden barrel held strips of dried salmon; another contained rusks. "Get yourself a cup of tea and some breakfast," Lukin said to Kurila. "We have a long day ahead."

Sava watched the forms of the oarsmen, still wrapped in their blankets on their beds of cut spruce boughs. "Those bums are still asleep."

The Company, for the last ten years or so, had been recruiting workers for the St. Michael district by means of an agreement with several Siberian prisons. Well-behaved convicts were released to the Company if they agreed to work a ten-year term in America. The deal had been struck as a cost-saving measure; the convict workers were paid only half the salary of free men, and after imperial taxes had been deducted they did not make enough to cover the cost of their tea, tobacco, sugar, and rum, which they had to purchase from the Company store. In theory one could do without these things, but it would make for a dreary life indeed. The upshot was that convict workers, in addition to being by and large the worst sort of men—murderers, thieves, and arsonists with no useful skills beyond pulling an oar or shoveling snow—almost always ended up deeply in debt to the Company. This in turn left them no choice but to re-up for another ten-year hitch. There was little sympathy in Lukin's heart for them, but such a system also meant that boat captains and bidarshiks were often stuck in perpetuity with a workforce of shiftless louts who generally required the lash for motivation.

Denisov rose and strode over to the man nearest the officers' camp and gave him a hard kick. The man bellowed and bolted to his feet, ready to take a swing at the owner of the foot, but he quickly shrank back into himself when he saw who it was. He glared at the fleet captain, but the bugs made it difficult to look anything but comical.

"You men get your lazy asses out of bed!" Denisov called. "We leave in twenty minutes, and any man who is not in his boat will be flogged." He took an idle sip of his tea. "If you doubt my word, you will not have a pleasant day."

He turned and walked back to the captains' fire. From somewhere in the stirring mass came a surly voice. "So easy for you, having your tea and smudge made for you by your boy!"

Denisov didn't break stride for his reply. "If you get up early you too can have your morning tea and smudge, Gospodin Lavrov."

"It's like this every year," Sava said, watching the men as they yawned and stretched and rubbed their faces.

Lukin grunted, reaching for another strip of dried salmon. "They should be a functioning boat crew by the time you get back to Nulato."

"It certainly would be nice," said Denisov, "if the Company would hire men who would work for something other than punishment."

The quarter moon still hung in the morning sky above the jagged line of spruce trees on the river's far bank. Faintly, in the blue skyshadow that sifted across her face something shifted. Lukin froze midway through his final sip of tea, watching as the moon's pale skin rippled into the old shapes, the iconography of the Kolosh people of New Archangel—the face and monstrous teeth and curled limbs of a being he'd long prayed would vanish from his world.

"You alright, Ivan?" Denisov asked across the fire.

"Yeah," Lukin mumbled. But all morning long he watched the water for what he knew was coming.

* * *

They pulled upriver all day without incident, then the next as well. The men grumbled and flexed their blistered hands, but there was nothing unusual in that. On the third afternoon they drew into a wide gravel beach at the mouth of the Nowikaket River. The village here was a major seasonal town in the spring and fall, before and after the Nuklukayet fair, but now it looked completely abandoned. Back in the birch trees, behind the head-high willows that sprouted from the sand, several dozen Denakeh houses made of poles and birchbark stood in a line facing the river.

Silence filled the town. There were only bird calls, the willow leaves riffling in the breeze. The faint buzz of yellowjackets in the willowtops. Then a dog started barking. It was joined by another.

They studied the scene from the boats at the shore. "What do you think?" Denisov asked Sava and Lukin.

Two dogs were tied to stakes by means of long poles attached to their collars with leather thongs. The animals lunged against these restraints, barking with their hackles up. They were not Russian sled dogs but the smaller hunting dogs kept by the locals.

"Someone must be feeding them," said Sava.

Lukin pointed. "I see fish on that drying rack."

Denisov went forward and retrieved his musket, powder horn and shot pouch from where they were stowed. He boosted himself over the bow onto the gravel beach. Sava followed suit with his own weapon. Lukin motioned to Kurila. "Bring your musket."

Kurila left his oar and went forward. Each man in the crew was armed in case of attack, but ammunition was strictly controlled by the captains. Kurila found his gun and hopped over the side. On the beach, they charged their weapons, all of British make purchased from the Hudson Bay Company at Fort Wrangell. Lukin poured a measure of gunpowder from his horn into Kurila's palm, then handed him a percussion cap between his thumb and forefinger.

"Ready?" said Denisov.

The others nodded. On Denisov's mark they raised their guns, pointed them skyward, and fired as one. The report punched out over the river. After a few heartbeats the birdsong returned in the slanted evening light. Then a figure emerged from the trees behind the house, moving slowly and gingerly.

"Looks like an old man," Sava said.

Denisov grunted. As they watched, the man stopped, raised a musket to his shoulder and fired back a return salute. This was the custom up and down the Kwifpak; to empty one's gun before entering a town showed peaceful intent.

Denisov and Lukin trudged across the gravel to the path through the willows and up to the town. The man was indeed old and his hair solidly gray. He walked with a pronounced limp. His left eye was milky and blue, with a deep scar cutting the eyebrow and down across both his wrinkled lips. He wore the usual Dinneh attire: leather moccasin-trousers and a long, fringed shirt with the tails shaped into steep points both front and back. Around his neck was a sheath holding a steel dagger with the pommel shaped into a pair of forked curls like the horns of a mountain ram.

He greeted them in the Denakeh language.

"Good evening," Lukin responded. He saw the man's eyes flick down to his own steel dagger that, as always, poked out from his waistcoat lapel. There was very little breeze and the mosquitoes were everywhere. "We haven't met. I'm Ivan Semyonovich Lukin, and this is Yosif Denisovich Denisov and Sava Matfeyovich Golinov."

They nodded at the elderly man. Both could get by in Denakeh when they had to, but Lukin was known far and wide as a master of languages, so by unspoken agreement they let him do the talking.

"I have seen these men before," the man said. "They live at Nulato." The dogs continued to bark. The man turned and shouted at them to be silent. Remarkably, they complied. He looked out at the boats. "You are bound for Nuklukayet."

"We are."

"I could not go this year." If he was disappointed to be left behind, he gave no indication of it.

"Looks like nobody else is here, Uncle."

"My granddaughter has stayed with me."

Just as he said this a woman walked out of the forest. She stood next to her grandfather. The evening was warm but she kept a shawl of beaver pelts clutched around her shoulders. Lukin tried to catch her eye, but she kept her gaze averted. Her free hand held a battered tin cup of water.

"We stayed behind to watch the houses," the old man said, which Lukin immediately understood as a euphemism. The various Dinneh tribes were wandering hunters and foragers in an exceedingly difficult country. The elderly often didn't fare well. It was not unheard of when food ran low in the winter for grandparents to volunteer to stay behind and let themselves freeze to death so their grandchildren could eat. He wondered, not so idly, if this man would be making that choice over the coming winter. They said that when death from freezing finally came all you would feel was warmth, as if you had just come from the cold into a house with a large fire burning.

Lukin reached into his shot pouch and withdrew a handful of musket balls, then from his pocket he took a twist of Chinese tobacco and a lump of vermilion. The flotilla kept a small box of such presents for occasions such as these. It was considered rude to show up at a house empty-handed.

"We have a few things for you, Uncle." Lukin handed over the gifts. The man's gun was an ancient-looking flintlock fitted with a Spanish miquelet action. God only knew how such an obscure firearm had made its way to the Kwifpak drainage.

He nodded his thanks.

Sava had been peering around at the girl. "Anfisa?"

Her eyes flicked up. "Hello, Sava."

"You know each other?" Lukin asked.

"Yes."

Denisov spoke up. "We had no idea you were here. Are you not going to the fair?"

"My husband drowned in the river last month."

Lukin noticed that her hair had been cut short, the universal sign of mourning among Dinneh people.

"Ah," said Denisov. "I am sorry to hear that."

She nodded, but wouldn't meet their eyes. Lukin found this a tad off-putting, but then again you weren't generally in a frame of mind to merrily entertain visitors when a loved one has just died. Lukin knew this up close from personal experience.

"Is there anything we can do?" Sava asked. He gestured at Lukin. "Captain Lukin here is a songleader, if perhaps you would like to recite some prayers."

Lukin was a trifle annoyed by having his time volunteered for him but decided not to make an issue of it.

"No, but thank you. He was not a Christian." Anfisa looked fully at Lukin for the first time as she spoke. He was surprised to see that she was in fact a Creole. There was a kerchief over her head, knotted under her chin, but you could see the Russian lines in her face and the tawny cast of her hair, or at least what remained of it. There was little else to be discerned, save the face that was lined with grief.

"You should stay the night," she said after a moment.

"Would that be alright?" Denisov said.

Her grandfather held out a hand to indicate the empty town. "We have lots of room."

On the way back to the boats, Lukin quietly said to Sava, "You know her?"

"She's Vasili Deryabin's daughter. His only surviving child."

"Deryabin?" The name was legendary along the Kwifpak, and indeed throughout the colony. He'd built Fort Nulato back in the 1830s—the post originally bore his name until it was subsumed by the more common usage of the name of the tributary stream next to it, Nulatokaket. Lukin had met him on a handful of occasions at St. Michael before his untimely death in the Battle of Nulato in 1851. He'd had been well-liked up and down the river, but when in his cups he had a dark, moody streak combined with a tendency to run his mouth nonstop that Lukin found off-putting. Natalia had avoided him whenever she could.

"What happened to the family after the Nulato fight?" Lukin asked.

"You never heard?" said Denisov.

"Only about a thousand different rumors. I didn't know any of his children even survived."

"Anfisa got away in the chaos. Chief Larion vowed to hunt her down, so she went into hiding here at Nowikaket."

"Seems like she wouldn't be that hard to find, living on the river."

"A shaman disguises her as an old woman whenever Larion is near," Sava said.

"Which shaman?"

"They call him Tathyaldin. He lives up the River Tananah. Her mother's family paid him to make the magic." Sava indicated the yellowjackets buzzing overhead in the willows. "They say that if you see lots of these meat bees, it's a sign that his magic is in effect."

"Hm," was all Lukin could come up with.

* * *

It was sometime in the small hours of the night when Lukin was driven awake by his old adversary insomnia. They'd moved into four of the Denakeh houses for the night, one for each boat crew and one for the captains. They were small and cramped by Russian standards, to say nothing of being dark and smoky with mice and voles rustling in the dim ecosystems of the far corners. But they did afford a space that could be closed off and smudged to drive away the bugs. And should rain come it was infinitely preferable to trying to sleep rolled up in a cold tarp in the wet sand.

He lay awake for some time, listening to the breathing and snores of Kurila and the others, then decided to get up and check on the boats. Out of long habit he'd memorized the layout of the house with respect to the best way to exit in the dim night without accidentally kicking someone awake. He folded his blanket back and crawled forward. Here and there a line of light came in between the birchbark sheets that comprised the walls and it gave him just enough to see where he was going.

Rain had fallen while they'd been sleeping though it appeared to have let up just a moment before. The fireweed and grass around the edge of the packed ground was thoroughly wet under his feet. The grace note was that with two other houses between him and the dogs he could step silently on the wet earth and not set them off.

The boats were safely tied up, but when rain came you really wanted to double and triple check things because water levels could rise drastically in a short time and nobody wanted to go swimming to retrieve a runaway boat. He hoped, somewhat forlornly, that he would be able to get back to sleep before morning.

The entire sky was covered over with cloud and the moon was nowhere to be seen but Lukin felt the shift in the air. He straightened up from the knot he was checking just as a form swirled in the water. Its head broke the surface and it stood and waded slowly into shore. The air was thick and damp and filled with the scent of rain.

"Hello, Zia," he said as she approached.

She smiled. "Ivan." She had the form of a fourteen-year-old girl without a stitch of clothing. Her hair was a wild mane of snarls and knots and rope-like clumps stuck together like felt that trailed to the backs of her knees. It was flecked with hemlock needles, salmon ribs, saltwater mussel shells, and bird feathers, though as ever it was not entirely clear if they were a random collection or had been planted there deliberately.

Lukin stood watching her for a long moment. "It's been a while."

The corner of her mouth turned up. "It took me some time to trace out where you went."

He thought of his daughter away at school. "Here," he said, starting to pull off his peajacket.

"How many times have I told you?" she said.

Lukin stopped, flattened his lips, shrugged the jacket back onto his shoulders.

"Come sit with me." She beckoned him to the very edge of the water. He knew it was a dangerous place to be with a creature such as this but he went anyway. She sat down and drew her knees up to her chest and wrapped her arms around them.

"You haven't aged a day," Lukin said.

She laughed a little. "You certainly have. Tell me where you were going."

"Why don't you let me help you?"

"I cannot be helped." She reached over and fingered the leather patch on the elbow of his jacket. "That Malimiut lady is still taking care of you?"

"My wife, you mean."

"I guess."

"She is." He drew in a breath and let it out as a sigh. "Things have been not well between us."

"Oh?"

They watched the river together while the tiniest of waves lapped at Zia's bare toes. Lukin kept his own feet back just far enough to not be wet.

"Some fish told me you are being sent on a quest," she said at length.

"Is that what it is?"

"That's what they said."

"What kind of fish were they?"

She shrugged. "I don't know. River fish."

"This isn't your country."

"You're my country. I feel like I'm losing you."

Lukin felt a disturbing combination of romantic lust and fatherly protection bubbling inside him. "You told me your mother was Kolosh. You should go back to that country."

"And my father was Russian."

He looked over at her, into the dark wells of her eyes, though he knew this was not a wise idea. "I want to help you, Zia. To set you free."

"There is no freedom for me."

"I could speak the name of your kind and destroy you."

"That's what the old people say. But we both know you won't do that."

I guess not, Lukin thought. This creature was a prisoner of her own being and he'd never found a way to manumit her from it, though God knew he'd tried. Then again, the only way that would happen would be if she found a human soul to devour, and she appeared to be interested only in his.

"I can show you more," she said.

"Alright."

She smiled a little from under her brow. The water splashed ever so slightly as she pushed herself back onto her knees. Lukin watched as she laid her palms onto the skin of the river and spread them slowly apart and the images took shape. There was a boy, maybe six or seven, dark hair and eyes, his clothes a ragged combination of Russian and Aleut make. A Creole with a familiar face, familiar because it looked very much like Lukin's and he knew this was his father, Semyon Lukin. He was scared, crying, surrounded by a crowd of jeering people Lukin recognized instantly as Kolosh—naked bodies, broad conical hats woven from split spruce roots. This was their town of enormous houses made of cedar posts and planks, painted with garish clan symbols. Beyond was a dark evergreen forest that rose vertically to the sodden clouds. The salient emotion that ran through him was terror followed by loneliness and loss.

There were other children, three of them. The crowd pushed them forward to the man who approached. His hat was more elaborate than the others' and the deference given to him was obvious at a glance. He stepped up to young Semyon and roughly gripped his face by the jaw to tilt his eyes up to him. The boy cried out as the man dug his thumb and forefinger into his cheeks to force open his mouth to submit his teeth for examination. The crowd chuckled and jeered, men, women, children. Dogs running everywhere. Then the man pried the boy's eyelids open with his fingers, one by one and examined the whites. Then he stepped back and whacked Semyon with a stick and gestured that he should enter the longhouse.

Lukin felt the flashes of blue and orange in his eyes and he pressed his hands to his face. He rolled onto his side, gasping until he found his voice. "This was Semyon. My father."

Zia had not moved from her kneeling position. "Yes."

"Taken as a slave."

"Yes."

Slowly he sat up again, rubbing his eyes with his sleeve. He opened his mouth to speak but she was peering around his head at the town.

"What is it?" Lukin asked, his voice still unsteady.

"You need to go to her."

"Who?"

"Is there some other woman in this town?"

You, he thought plaintively.

"You know what I am, Ivan." She stabbed a finger toward the houses. "Now go."

He rose and walked through the willows, peering ahead to see what she'd been pointing at. He looked back once and there was only the tail of a river otter sliding into the water and no tracks to indicate that Zia had been there at all.

It was in Lukin's nature to be silent, even when there was no obvious reason to do so. It was something his Deghitan uncles had impressed upon him, that stillness was a pleasure. He knew the rain would not return any time soon because the yellowjackets were back at work. He paused a moment to watch them with his head craned back as they buzzed their way from leaf to leaf, wondering about Zia and what she could have meant.

Back next to the old man's house the dogs started barking. This was nothing unusual in itself and normally he wouldn't have paid it any mind, but Zia had certainly seemed agitated.

He'd just come out of the willows when he heard a noise that sounded very much like a low wail. It was unmistakably the cry of a woman, and as Zia had said there was only one woman in the empty town.

He stopped, put a hand up to his ear to hear better. The dogs continued, making the nippy *rowrowrowrow* bark peculiar to hunting dogs.

Lukin turned his head a little, then heard another pleading cry, followed by a Denakeh word: "*No!*" Then another wail that was cut off in a strangling gargle.

His pulse quickened as he moved. Coming around the corner of the nearest house the first thing he saw was Anfisa on the ground. On top of her was Lavrov, one hand at her throat and the other fumbling with his trousers as he used his knees to force her leg open. Lavrov's eyes met Lukin's. Lukin charged straight for him but was stopped in his tracks when Anfisa's grandfather leapt from behind the nearest house, yanked Lavrov's chin up by his beard and reached around with his long dagger. He'd rolled up his sleeves to accommodate this task.

"Stop!" Lukin shouted, thrusting out a palm.

The old man looked up and Lavrov took advantage of the pause to sink his teeth into his forearm, simultaneously driving a hard elbow back into his ribs. The man grunted and crumpled as Lavrov bolted for the woods.

"Sava!" Lukin called. "Yosif!" The dogs were lunging on the ends of their tethers. Anfisa curled up on the ground. Her grandfather staggered to his feet as Lukin sprinted after Lavrov. The convict threw a glance over his shoulder and it slowed him just enough that Lukin was able to gain a step on him. He lunged, clipping him down by the backs of his knees. Lavrov came up cursing and stabbed a thumb at Lukin's eye to gouge it out but Lukin rabbit-punched the steel pommel of his dagger into the side of Lavrov's head like a makeshift brass knuckles. Lavrov went limp for a moment which gave Lukin time to flip him over and get a knee into the small of his back while pressing his neck down against the ground. He held him there, pinned like a chicken on the chopping block as both Sava and Denisov rushed from the house with their muskets, followed by a crowd of oarsmen. All were blinking and sleepy in the four am daylight.

"What's going on here?" Denisov demanded.

"I caught this bag of guts trying to violate Madame Deryabina." He had no idea what her married name was, or if she'd even changed it and there was no time in the moment to inquire.

Her grandfather was kneeling next to her with a tender hand upon her shoulder. Denisov hunkered down next to them. "He tried to force you, Anfisa?"

She seemed incapable of speech. He repeated the question to the old man in his halting Denakeh. He nodded once. Blood ran down his arm where he'd been bitten. He rose painfully and hobbled over to Lavrov, still holding his dagger. "You would do best to move away," he said to Lukin who was still on top of the perpetrator.

Lukin shook his head. Somehow he managed to maintain his composure despite Lavrov's writhing and kicking. "Uncle," he said, "I ask that you allow us to deal out Russian justice to this animal. He is of my crew and is my responsibility. I cannot allow you to cut his throat."

The old man fixed Lukin with a very hard, level look. Among the Dinneh tribes it was the supreme test of manhood to kill a grizzly bear with a spear, and Lukin knew instantly that this man had done so, probably several times. The scars across his face no doubt told the story, but then so did his remaining eye.

"Petroski and Yarko," Lukin said, still struggling against Lavrov, who had taken to snarling like a rabid wolf.

The only two non-Russian men in the crew came forward, one a Pole, the other a Finlander. Both rowed in Sava's boat.

"Help me stand him up," Lukin ordered. Together the three of them pulled Lavrov to his feet. Yarko the Finlander twisted his arm up between his shoulder blades. Once he was upright, Denisov stood face to face with him. He pointed at Anfisa. "Just what in hell is wrong with you?"

By way of answer, Lavrov reared back and spat an enormous gob of snot into Denisov's face. "Fuck all you halfbreed Creoles!"

Denisov raised his sleeve to his face and deliberately wiped away the expectorate. This done, he smacked his palm across Lavrov's face. The convict's head was not fully traveled from the force of this blow when Denisov returned a fierce backhand that clapped him hard enough that blood and spittle flew from his mouth.

"You can't whip me," Lavrov protested through his mangled lips. "Flogging is illegal now!"

"Lavrov, you are an animal, so we will deal with you as an animal."

"Suck my cock, mongrel. I may be a convict, but I'm still a white man. God and the Czar himself cannot make you more than me!"

"God is up in Heaven," Denisov said with an unfriendly smile, leaning closer so he was looking straight into Lavrov's eyes, "and the Czar is far away." He turned his face to the sky, gauging the amount of light. "Captain Lukin."

"Yes."

"Would you cut a willow switch?"

"With pleasure."

Down in the willows he found a nice seven-footer, big enough that he needed both hands to wield it. Why carry a lash when green switches were to be had everywhere for the cutting? He put away his dagger in its sheath around his neck and drew his smaller belt knife, whittling beaverwise around the wand's base where it curled out of the main trunk of an older stump. It came free with a snap. Once stripped of its leaves and twigs it rippled like a buggy whip.

They had Lavrov stripped to the waist and lashed to a birch tree with his knees on the ground and his face pressed up against the trunk. Mosquitoes crawled over his exposed flesh like a living carpet. Lukin got the impression the other men held no love for Lavrov, but then convicts from the hard labor camps on the Lena River were probably incapable of feeling such things as love. Lukin pointed the switch and inclined his head toward their mendicant. Denisov nodded.

The men stood with their arms crossed over their chests or their thumbs hooked into their belts or vest pockets. A couple took the time to light their pipes. Off to the side he saw Kurila looking uncomfortable and pensive, suddenly just a boy among men.

"Friends," Lukin said to the old man and Anfisa, who stood next to Sava. Her grandfather looked up, though the widow still clutched her robe and seemed on the point of collapse. "I promise you I shall not go easy on him." He held out the long switch and waggled the supple tip. "I will caress him until he can no longer scream."

"All I ask," Denisov said, "is that he be fit to row."

Lukin assumed his stance. Several of the mosquitoes took flight and he saw that the man's back was a grayish mass of scarred-over whipping stripes, welts and puckers that no doubt spoke a long litany of subhuman behavior. Above the old scars, across the top of his shoulders, he was surprised to discover a command tattooed in, of all things, Slavonic, the sacred language of the Church: Flog Well and Do Your Duty.

Lavrov's eyes rolled around to watch him, filled with hate and challenge.

"As you request," Lukin said to him in the language of his tattoo. He set both hands on the base of the switch and delivered the first stripe. Lavrov jerked and twisted against his bonds. Lukin drew the switch back slowly to take a careful aim, then sliced him again. And again. At first there were only red welts to be seen, but as the switch landed again and again, swishing the air with each stroke, the skin and scar tissue opened and the blood ran. For a time, Lavrov kept his eyes open to glare at Lukin, but as the whipping continued his head slumped and his gaze sank.

Finally, Lukin halted and wiped the sweat from his brow. The bark of the slender willow was shredded, hanging off and dripping blood. Lavrov breathed in slow heavy draws.

Lukin turned to face the boat crews. "Every man of you look here," he said in what was unmistakably the voice of a bidarshik, a voice even Denisov was inclined to defer to. "If any of you have thoughts of molesting Native or Creole women, this will happen to you. And if any of you hold the opinion that we Creoles are less than you because of the color of our skin, you would do well to remember that we are the free citizens of this colony, both in practice and in law. You are laborers sent here because you were not wanted where you came from. This is our country, and you will address your captains and the local people with nothing but the utmost respect and courtesy."

He lifted the bloody switch for all to see. "If any man wishes to express such opinions as Gospodin Lavrov here, let him speak now."

Nobody spoke.

Lavrov had slumped down, limp with pain so that the ropes dug into his flesh.

"As for you," Lukin said to him, "if you ever again address me or any Creole of my acquaintance as a *mongrel*, I will personally cut your tongue out and feed it to the seagulls." He slid the butt end of the makeshift whip under Lavrov's chin and pushed his head up to force the man to look at him. "Do you doubt my word?"

"No," Lavrov whispered.

"Good." Lukin let his head drop. Administering a flogging was hard work, and there was a scrim of sweat between his shirt and the skin beneath. He ran a hand over his wet hair. "Cut him loose and get him ready to row."

* * *

"Ivan," said Neofit, pounding a fist on the desk, "You're squandering what little food we have left!"

Spring had come late to the Kuskokwim in 1860, with a superabundance of rain. There was still ice over the river at the start of June, something nobody could recall ever happening before. And as if that were not enough, the king salmon failed to arrive. A country already impoverished from a long winter and a late spring, when food was in short supply during any normal year, was left bereft of the summer bounty it relied on. Some claimed it was because of the late breakup that the salmon had refused to come. Others, particularly the local Kitagmiut who lived on the downriver side of Fort Kolmakov were certain it was the work of a malevolent Koltsan shaman who lived up near the forks. Lukin was unsurprised by this; the Kitagmiut like all the coastal people were ancient enemies of the inland Dinneh tribes. And then there were the Christianized locals. There seemed to be no end to the converts—usually elderly women—who stopped him every day to wag a finger at his face and lecture that God himself was angry at all the Kuskokwim people for permitting shamanism to flourish despite His teachings.

Ivan Lukin had been the bidarshik for not quite five years with a track record that was average at best. He wasn't the worst fort manager who ever lived, but he certainly wasn't the best, and he was keenly aware of the fact that his father had set the standard by which the Company judged all trading captains. Expectations for him were high, and those expectations were nowhere more evident than here in his office with his brother-in-law glaring at him over his desk.

Lukin leaned back in his chair and tossed his pen into the gutter of the notebook he'd been working in. He rubbed his eyes with his thumb and forefinger. "Just what do you suggest I do, Fita?"

"Gather what food we can find and send some hunters downriver for caribou." Neofit flung a hand in the general direction of the refugee camp that had accumulated around the fort. "And quit playing favorites by giving so much food to the Ingalit." Like a lot of people he insisted on using this word for the Deghitan. "The Kitagmiut are about to riot and storm the fort."

"How fortunate for them that you're their kin," Lukin said, "their man on the inside."

Neofit planted his palms on the desk between them. "You love the Dinneh too much, Ivan. These people know where your loyalties lie." Among the reasons Semyon Lukin had chosen this particular site for a trading station was that it lay right at the boundary where the Kitagmiut and Dinneh worlds met. It had been a smart commercial decision, but now it was becoming more and more of a liability as the Kitagmiut and the Deghitan—whose relations were largely a history of murder, ambush, and slave raids—crowded around the fort in makeshift camps. And it fell to Lukin the younger to somehow manage this whole mess.

"You would do well to control your tongue, Fita. You may be family, but I will have you flogged if you force me."

Neofit's waistcoat hung loose on his reduced frame beneath his jacket. Everyone's clothes were fitting slack, even Lukin's. "The men want to go down to look for caribou."

"The men will do whatever I tell them to do, regardless of what they want." He felt less certain than ever that he could keep command of things, but it was what Semyon would have said. "If there were caribou to be found downriver, the Kitagmiut would have word of it. And I will not sentence our families to even more privation just so you and your friends can go on some wild goose chase."

Neofit folded his arms over his chest. "I'm not the one who was just gone four days on a goose hunt and came back empty-handed."

It was true. Even the ducks and geese seemed to be avoiding the area. He'd only seen three mallards the whole time, streaking by well out of range. No open water, after all, meant no waterfowl.

"I run things here, not you." It sounded defensive and petty. This was maybe the worst part of a famine, it came to him. No, the worst part was quite obviously the hunger, then seeing the distended bellies of the small children, your own children in particular.

He rested his elbows on the desk that had once been his father's and drew a long breath. Hunger made everything a slog, especially trying to think straight.

Neofit pulled back and strode for the door. He paused with his hand on the latch, as if about to speak.

"I am hungry too," Lukin said. "But the fish will come eventually. The ducks and caribou too."

"You have run out of friends, Ivan." Neofit pulled the door open. "Do not flatter yourself by thinking you are infallible just because you're Semyon's son."

Lukin had to bite his tongue to keep from swearing at him. If he thought managing all this was so damned easy, let him try it himself. His mother had often told him that only a fool insists on having the last word in an argument, though he suspected this may have been a parental tactic to shut his mouth.

"Get out."

"No."

Lukin rose from his chair. "I beg your pardon."

"I have thirty armed men outside. I came in here to give you one last chance, but you refused to listen to reason. So you are no longer in command of this fort."

"Bullshit."

"Go and see."

Lukin regarded Neofit for a long moment, then crossed the room and pulled the edge of the door from his hand. A ring of hard-looking men—Kitagmiut, Russian, and Creole—had formed in a horseshoe around his office in the fort's muddy courtyard. All were armed with muskets, lances, or bows.

He stepped outside. "What is this?"

Nobody spoke. Neofit came out behind him. "This is me relieving you of command, Ivan."

Lukin knew he'd already spent too much time talking. He spun and clocked Neofit square on the mouth. Neofit staggered back and Lukin stepped into him, hitting him in the gut and trying to shove him back against the wall of the building. Neofit slipped a third swing by ducking under Lukin's arm and punching him square in the kidney. Pain exploded through his abdomen and he tried to spin around but Neofit swept his leg out from under him and he went straight down to the sloppy dirt. Lukin was weak from hunger and it took the breath right out of him. Instinct alone forced him to his feet but Neofit drove a knee into his stomach and he went down again. Finally he found a full breath and launched himself at his midsection. It bowled him over onto his back with Lukin punching hard at his solar plexus then snatching up a stick of scrap lumber pressed into the mud. He cocked it to swing at Neofit's head but a hand from behind snatched it away. Lukin turned to see who had dared interfere and this gave Neofit just enough slack to jump up and deliver a savage kick to his face.

There were stars in his vision and he had a vague recollection of hitting the ground again. They were both panting and sputtering for breath when Neofit dragged him to his feet and shoved him face-first against the log wall of his office. "You should have kept more food for yourself instead of giving it to your aunts and uncles," he hissed into Lukin's ear. "It might have given you the strength to fight."

Lukin tried to struggle, but there was nothing left.

"Get me that line!" Neofit barked to the crowd. Someone handed him a length of moosehide thong and two Kitagmiut men held Lukin against the wall while Neofit lashed his hands behind him. They frogmarched him to the octagonal guardhouse and shoved him inside. Later in the day the door opened and Iriana and Ilya where pushed through. A workman held a pistol on Lukin while another cut his bonds. Iriana sank down to the floor against the wall while he flexed his fingers and tried to shake some feeling back into them. Ilya came over to him and he hugged him, whispering to him that it would be alright and trying not to think of Anastasia at school, or about how he could feel his son's ribs under his clothes as he patted his back. *The family that is imprisoned together stays together,* he thought. The irony brought a snort of laughter to his lips.

"What?" Iriana whispered.

"Nothing." Looking back, he could see this as the beginning of them not talking to one another anymore.

Three days later, the door opened and someone set a bowl of cold roasted caribou meat on the floor. Lukin was too hungry to care that Neofit had been right.

3

THE ERRAND DRAWS NIGH — A STORM — THE DEVIL YOU KNOW — DERYABIN'S ETERNAL SEARCH — ARRIVAL AT THE NUKLUKAYET TRADING GROUND — JOIN THE NAVY — GREETING THE CUSTOMERS — TANANAH SHAMAN — HOW TO READ SIGN — CONSIDERATIONS — A DINNEH FROLIC — COMMERCE BEGINS — STICKING POINT — FAMILY HISTORY — THE PRICE TO BE PAID

Their progress up the River Kwifpak was marked by the mouths of the rivers and creeks they camped at. They rowed every day, even Lavrov, who kept his eyes down and appeared to have learned a lesson in life, at least for the time being. Regarding his behavior, Sava said to Lukin one morning around their fire at the mouth of the Melozikaket River that a dog never stops looking for the easy way out.

Twice they were passed by Denakeh families on their way upriver for the fair. They had only two or three paddles in each of these craft, but they carried nowhere near the tonnage of the Russian boats and could outpace them easily.

Day by day they drew closer, and Lukin could feel the risky nature of his errand looming ahead.

Just before Nuklukayet they rowed into a thunderstorm. Lightning crackled across the sky and thunder boomed so hard they could see tiny ripples across the current from each explosion. Contrary winds surged to and fro across the water and even across the distance to shore you could see the silvery undersides of the willow leaves flashing in the tempest.

Denisov's boat, as always, was in the lead. He whistled across the water for the captains' attention, then gave the hand signal to put into shore, a prudent course of action considering all the iron, lead, and copper they carried. Quite suddenly their cargo was just a bundle of lightning magnets, to say nothing of the water that inevitably sloshed around beneath the floorboards and the river all around them. Both trailing boats followed their admiral to a gravel bar on the downstream end of an island covered in spruce timber. Working fast as the first big drops stained the gravel, they anchored and tied the boats off to shore. Each crew scuttled to the protection of the spruce trees where the thick boughs overhead created a circle of dry ground beneath each trunk. Censers were lit, for the mosquitoes sought the shelter of the trees as well.

"Yes!" said Yarko the Finlander when the smoke began to fill the air beneath the boughs. He shook a steely fist at the fleeing insects. "Drive them out into the rain to die!" Everyone had a chuckle at his not-so-fake glee, even the captains.

The oarsmen loved these thunder breaks, for it gave them a chance to smoke and loaf and catch up on their sleep. They were stuck in place until the storm moved on, but it was no respite for the officers.

"Damn this storm," Denisov said, peering out at the sheets of rain that hammered the forest and pummeled their boats. "I had high hopes we'd beat the Hudson Bay men to the fair this year."

Lukin looked over at him, thinking about all the years Denisov and Sava had spent on this river, with him a newcomer. There was a question of why Vakrameev and the governor had not sent one of them. Denisov despite his years of school had never learned to read or write properly, something Lukin knew quite well because he'd spent hours trying to help him with the lessons in New Archangel. Sava, however, was a fair hand at writing and was perfectly capable of penning a report to the Company's managers.

"The ice goes out on the upper river far earlier than it does around Nulato," Sava said. "And they have the advantage of the downstream current."

"That would be hard to beat," Lukin said.

"And every hour we tarry on shore," said Sava, "is an hour we're not at Nuklukayet buying furs."

Denisov grunted. The rumpled booming of thunder sounded across the world again and the rain came down even harder. *We're gonna have to bail those boats before we continue,* Lukin thought. Rudinov had pulled out his tarot deck and was giving a reading to Petroski the Pole.

"Tell me," Lukin said.

Denisov looked over at him.

"You reckon Larion will be there?"

"I presume so. Why do you ask?"

Lukin let his eyes travel over to Kurila who sat leaning against a tree and staring out at the rain.

"He'll be fine," Denisov said. "Larion comes to Nulato a lot in the winter. This won't be the first time they've been around one another since the battle."

"Larion's a troublemaker," Lukin said. "We were even on alert at Fort Kolmakov for a year after he sacked Nulato." It had in fact led to Natalia's death, though he'd forced himself for years not to blame Larion for it. "Why do you keep letting him trade at Nulato?"

"He's one of the most powerful chiefs in the Interior," Denisov said. "Even if we could declare him persona non grata, he'd just take his custom upriver to the British."

"Is there a worry he might come back to Nulato looking for trouble?"

"It's not impossible."

"I guess the devil you know is better than the one you don't."

"Besides," said Sava, "he's a man with enemies. That makes him easy to steer if you know which levers to pull."

Denisov knocked the ashes from his pipe into his palm and tossed them out into the rain. "Someone told me you're related to him."

"Larion?" said Lukin.

"Mm."

"It's true."

Denisov and Sava watched him as the rain intensified yet again. Another thunderclap rolled across the river.

"Our mothers were of the same clan," Lukin was focused on refilling his pipe. The silence from the direction of the crewmen drew his attention in that direction, and the other captains followed his look. The men had clustered around Rudinov as he tapped a rough finger on a card. He glanced up and caught the eye of the officers.

"What idolatry are you peddling over there, Rudinov?" Denisov asked over the sound of the rain.

Rudinov looked up without moving his finger. "Tarechenko here asked about Captain Deryabin's boat, sir."

Lukin caught the look that Sava and Denisov exchanged. "What is it?" he asked.

Sava's eyes moved away. Denisov frowned. "Rudinov claims to have seen Deryabin's ghost piloting a boat upriver."

"It's quite a story," Sava mumbled.

Tarechenko and Rudinov and the others watched them. Lukin coughed. "I haven't heard this tall tale," he said to Rudinov, who hadn't moved.

"It's no tall tale, Captain. I saw it with my own two eyes. Near the mouth of the Melozikaket."

"I think you've either said too much or too little."

Rudinov looked around at his fellow crewmen, of which he was the eldest. He'd been out in the forest hunting ptarmigan when Larion and his fighters struck Nulato on their way to the nearby Denakeh winter town. He'd come back to find the burned hulk of the fort and the bodies full of arrows and run through with lances. Hacked to pieces with axes. Vasili Deryabin and his wife had been among them, though his daughter Anfisa got away into the forest. Rudinov was the only surviving member of the original Nulato crew.

He frowned a little. "It was six years ago, summer of '56. Back when Hudson Bay first started coming down to Nuklukayet. Metrikov was still only sending one boat, and we were coming back downriver after trading."

The sky lit up with a silent flash of lightning. Two seconds later the thunder cracked like a whip so hard a couple of the men, including Sava and Lukin, jumped. Rudinov remained unfazed. "We came around the last bend in the river before you see the Melozi and there they were."

"They?" said Lukin.

"Captain Deryabin with a boat crew. Rowing upriver."

Lukin waited for him to continue.

"They were skeletons with rags of clothes and rawhide flesh," Rudinov said. "The living dead pulling on splintered oars."

"How do you know it was Deryabin then?"

"I would know that man in death or in life." Rudinov held Lukin's eyes for several heartbeats before continuing. "He turned and looked right at us as we passed. His oarsmen were Cossacks from the old days, from back before Baranov and Shelhikov. The old freebooters who butchered whole villages of Aleuts and raped their women and cut fingers and toes and ears off their children."

Lukin was unsure what to say of this. Strange things happened in the forest and on the rivers. Anyone in the colony knew this.

"Captain Denisov there was in the boat with us," Rudinov said. "Every man aboard saw it."

All eyes moved to Denisov. "What do you make of it?" Lukin asked him.

He could see in Denisov's eyes that he wanted to deny having seen this vision of death, but then he reluctantly picked up the thread. "The cargo they carried was bones. Bones and skulls from every beast in the forest and the sea. Piled so high amidships it looked like it would swamp their vessel at any moment."

Lightning flashed again, then the thunder filled the air. Nobody moved. When the rumble had faded, Denisov looked away. "God's work is shown to men in many different forms."

Rudinov shifted back onto his knees and folded his arms over his chest. "What we do here is not God's work. Captain Deryabin was a merry man, but he was also a brooding one. There were ugly things in his past, and the search for the British fort upriver consumed his entire soul."

The rain continued to slash the river; here it was so wide the far bank was little more than a dark stripe of trees. Sava cleared his throat. "They say he's been damned to search forever on the river for the British fort."

Lukin's pipe had gone cold in his hand. He studied the lines of Rudinov's face.

"We're all damned to search forever, Captain," Rudinov said.

* * *

They smelled Nuklukayet before they caught sight of it. The wind blew downriver and carried with it a cloud of wood and gudge smoke, the accumulated burnings of several hundred people camped in the same place for an extended time. Before long it became visible as a bluish haze hanging over the water, then they came around the final bend and the steep shoreline of the south bank peeled away into a vast sandbar, the result of the endless sediment carried down and dumped by the Tananah River.

The beach was filled with birchbark canoes beyond counting. There were the domed caribou-skin tents of the Quarrelers from upriver, the conical teepee-like tents of the Denakeh, and lean-tos of every size and configuration. Smokehouses and fish-drying racks stood everywhere for curing the bounty of salmon brought in by the submerged forest of fish traps staked to the shore. In the spruce woods behind the camping ground a profusion of cache platforms were built between the trunks to store food, hides, and furs beyond the reach of bears, foxes, and dogs. The dogs in particular were everywhere, darting among the tents and fire pits as people gathered down by the water to greet the new arrivals.

Denisov pushed his fingertips into the corners of his mouth and whistled at the other two boats. Lukin looked over to see him raise both arms with the palms facing inward, then bring them together. He repeated this three times. It was the signal for all three boats to close up the distance between them.

"Let's tighten it up," Lukin said to his crew. They continued the upstream stroke, drawing in next to Sava within easy voice communication of Denisov.

People were assembling along the water's edge. Most of the men carried muskets at the ready, waiting.

"Rudinov," Lukin said, "you and Kurila go forward and ready the gun."

Each of the three boats was equipped with a two-pound brass swivel cannon at the bow. All been loaded that morning with a blank charge. Kurila and Rudinov shipped their oars and moved carefully up to the bow. Rudinov opened a tarred birchbark box and withdrew the coil of fusecord. Kurila fished his flint and steel from his vest pocket and struck a spark onto the charred end of the coil. When it caught, he blew on the end to get it glowing, then Rudinov clamped the smoldering cord into a screw vise fixed to the end of a three-foot pole. Kurila held it well away from the touchhole as Rudinov aimed the gun up into the air.

"Ready here," he said when he was satisfied.

"On my mark," Denisov called, holding his hand up in the air. The gunners in the other boats waited.

"Fire!"

The gunners touched the fuses to their pieces. Three charges fired as one, sending out a plume of sulfur smoke and fire, a flat boom that rolled over the river to the bank and back again. The recoil rocked each boat.

"Reload," Denisov ordered. Rudinov had a wad of wet moss wound onto the swabbing worm. This he ran down the barrel to extinguish any smoldering sparks. Kurila poured in a measure of gunpowder and Rudinov held the fuse at a safe distance as the youth rammed home the charge with a tight wadding fashioned of wood shavings and twine.

On the bank the crowd of Dinneh men raised their muskets to their shoulders and returned the salute with a deafening fusillade. The smoke from their guns drifted across the river to mix with that of the cannon.

"Ready here," came the call from each of the gunners.

Denisov had his hand in the air again. "Fire!"

Again the gunners fired. The men on shore had reloaded. They shouldered their muskets and fired a second return. The four men remaining at their oars in each boat had to work continuously to keep the boats in place against the current.

They repeated the salute three more times. Smoke and a smell of rotten eggs filled the air.

"That's enough," Denisov finally called after the fifth round. "Let's go in."

Yarko the Finlander had been moved over to Lukin's boat to trade out for Lavrov. "Seems like a waste of gunpowder," he said.

"Not really," Lukin replied. "Every shot they fire means more powder they buy from us."

"I do love shooting that cannon," Kurila piped up as he settled back at his oar.

"Join the navy, son," said the man behind him with a laugh. "You can shoot cannons all day long and sail the seven seas into the bargain."

Lukin chuckled. "Just make sure you save enough powder for the muskets."

Many hands make for light work, and several Dinneh men shucked off their moccasin pants and waded bare-legged into the frigid silty water to help land the Russian boats. Once they were secured and made fast to the beach, the captains moved through the crowd, shaking hands and clapping backs, giving respectful greetings to their favorite ladies and their children. The mob had formed a loose ring around them and Denisov and Sava had to gently push their way over to Lukin.

"Will you do the honors?" Denisov quietly asked Lukin in Russian. "I hate giving speeches."

"You're half Kolosh, Ivan," Lukin whispered back. "You Kolosh Creoles are supposed to be first-rate orators."

"I didn't get that half in the breeding."

"Alright," Lukin agreed. "But you owe me a double drink of rum tonight."

"I'll take that deal."

Every man, woman, and child in the camp had formed into the crowd around them, along with the pack of hunting dogs that yapped at the newcomers until cuffed by their owners or whoever was standing nearby. Chastised, they sniffed the air, growling quietly until they were kicked off to the outer edge. Everywhere was fringe on pointed shirttails, beads, bands of dyed porcupine quills, and strips of otter and mink fur. Many of the younger girls had taken to tying white dentalia seashells from the coast with small bird feathers to the very tips of their long hair with strands of sinew. The young downriver men had rubbed grease and red clay into their hair until it was stiff and shiny, then wrapped the burly locks into a thick queue down their backs that left an oily stain on their shirts.

"There's Larion," Denisov said, nodding his head in the direction of the infamous chief.

"Look at that British coat Sinateh is wearing," Sava said in a low voice. The garment of which he spoke was cut of scarlet wool with silver buttons, braid, and epaulets, worn open in front over his leather shirt. This was a man Lukin knew by reputation only—he was the principal chief of the Quarrelers and had built his power base as a middleman trader, selling guns, blankets, and beads to the most distant of tribes.

"That looks like an officer's coat," Lukin said, keeping his face in a genial smile for the crowd. The two chiefs were moving through, coming to greet the traders. "Do you think the British army is here on the river?"

"You'll find out soon," whispered Denisov. "Sinateh," he said in a louder voice. "And Larion. It's good to see both of you."

Both chiefs wore elaborately beaded leather shirts with fringe. Sinateh's hair was clubbed and queued at the base of his neck, wrapped with strands of beads and seashells and the tail-fan a sharptail grouse. The center lobe of his nose was pierced and through this hole he wore a pair of tailfeathers from a pintail duck that stuck out well past his cheeks. Larion despite his age affected the more current hairstyle of ochre and grease twisted into ropes. He had it all piled up into a large bun atop the crown of his head. His face was tattooed with black lines to record the enemies he'd vanquished. Kurila's parents were among them.

Larion spoke first. "Little cousin, it's good to see you as well. I always wonder if I will pass you Russians on the way up here but I never do."

"We're a lazy bunch," Lukin said affably. "We always start much later than you."

Larion put out his hand to shake. Most of the Dinneh, and especially those who'd had little contact with whitemen, regarded this custom with suspicion. The prevailing wisdom was that if you clasped a man's hand it was too easy for him to yank you off balance and stick a knife into you. Leaders like Larion and Sinateh had made their peace with it but preferred to perform the ritual at the end of pleasantries rather than at the first greeting.

Lukin took the proffered hand and shook. He turned to Sinateh. "I hope you haven't sold all your furs to the British like I'm told you did last year."

Sinateh was stern and taciturn, even for a Dinneh man. He was not quite arrogant, but did strike Lukin as the sort of fellow who took himself a bit too seriously. Then again he was far and away the most powerful man on the upper river and his good grace was very much in the Company's interest, particularly in light of Lukin's upcoming espionage mission.

The Quarreler language was beyond his comprehension, but then he'd already figured out that when the giant whose name sounded like aspen leaves had spoken to him as a child, he'd only said that Lukin would understand all the languages of the country. The Quarrelers, evidently, lived in a land beyond that large man's ken.

Sinateh spoke in thickly-accented Denakeh. "I have heard of you, Lukin. I look forward to seeing what sort of fine things you have brought us."

"Always so formal, my friend," Denisov said.

"I return whatever is given to me."

Lukin pursed his lips and nodded. He was about to mention that he would like to speak to the chief later about some confidential business when there came a shout from behind the crowd and folks parted to allow through a third chieftain.

"Who's this?" he whispered to Denisov in Russian.

"I don't know."

Larion, who spoke fair Russian, stepped in next to Lukin. "His name is Tathyaldin." He pointed in the direction of the Tananah River. "He's from way up in the mountains, near the base of Dinalee."

The name Tathyaldin meant nothing to Lukin until he recalled what was said at Nowikaket about the shaman who disguised Anfisa Deryabina as an old woman. He had the look of someone straight out of the forest, as did the contingent of Tananah people who filled in behind him. Sinateh wore the scarlet military style jacket, and both he and Larion had Chinese beads sewn onto their clothes. They owned steel knives, muskets, and axes; their wives cooked in copper kettles. Tathyaldin's attire, and that of his followers, bore not a trace of anything manufactured. Their clothing was painted with dyes made from earth and plants, and trimmed with the bands of woven porcupine quills that nowadays were considered rather old-fashioned by the tribes of the Kwifpak. The men carried bows and quivers of arrows. These had been brought to the river's edge, Lukin surmised, to show that even though they had no guns to fire off, they were not unarmed.

Tathyaldin's face was painted yellow with black patches around his eyes and mouth and a black line down the center of his nose. A substantial ring of hammered copper hung from his septum. Lukin felt a buzz and whir of air against his ear. He shied away slightly as the yellowjacket zipped around to hover in front of his face, then moved over to Denisov and then to Sava.

Regaining his composure, Lukin looked back at Tathyaldin, who was studying him openly. The yellowjacket departed as suddenly as it had appeared.

"Fucking meat bees," Sava muttered.

"There haven't been any Tananah people here for a few years," Denisov said into Lukin's ear. "They say he gets seized by animal spirits when food is scarce and they tell him where to find game."

"That's a talent I wish I had."

Tathyaldin stepped directly up to Sava, then over to Denisov, peering at each one of them as if they were animals tied to a stake. He said something in a loud voice, spoken to no one in particular. It had the timbre of a demand. When Lukin cocked an ear to try and catch it all he heard was something about somebody bringing something in the past tense, but could discern no more than that. It was often like this when he encountered a new language; he had to listen carefully to see if it was included in the giant's prophecy from long ago. *All the languages of the country* was, after all, a somewhat vague category. But he was hopeful, given that little snippet of comprehension.

Larion translated. "He wants to know who brought these Kolosh to a neutral spot like Nuklukayet." The Kolosh people of the coastal rainforests were regarded by the Dinneh with a mix of fear and respect for their sharp trading. It was not unheard of for their war captains to lead slave raids into the far Interior, but then the Kolosh were also the principal merchants of the slender white dentalia seashells that the Dinneh coveted as the very mark of success in life.

Lukin looked over at his fellow captains, both with heavy Kolosh lineage.

Denisov shrugged. "It's a sharp eye he has."

"Tananah people have not been on friendly terms with the Kolosh lately," Sinateh said. Lukin got the distinct impression he was speaking in euphemisms.

The Tananah chief stood back and regarded Lukin. He spoke a few lines; Lukin heard the word *trade*, and some intimation that Lukin was not Kolosh.

"He says you're not Kolosh," Larion said. "So he will trade with you."

Lukin guessed the man's age at somewhere around thirty, though it was hard to tell with all the paint. He also reckoned the odds at about fifty-fifty that he was either a reliable supplier of peltry or completely full of shit. The trading fair at Nuklukayet had been happening every summer for many generations before the Russians or British arrived in the country, and Tananah folk were hardly something new, but Lukin knew very little about them. The Denakeh and Quarrelers seemed to regard them as unsophisticated wildmen. He'd heard that the bands along the lower reaches of their river had been hit hard by influenza a few years before. There was also a persistent rumor that they were cannibals. Lukin didn't put much stock in that, but it was telling that not even Larion dared venture up the Tananah River. He also recalled Sava once saying that the Tananah Indians didn't always come down to Nuklukayet, but when they did, they brought top quality furs.

"Big Cousin," Lukin said to Larion, "could you tell him that I'm glad he and his people are here, and I look forward to trading with him." When this had been translated, he turned his attention to the rest of the crowd, still speaking Denakeh. "We look forward to trading with all of you. We've brought you many fine things from Nulato."

* * *

There was a patch of ground on the riverbank reserved for Russian and British traders. Lukin took Kurila with him to study the area while the boats were being unloaded.

"Wood chips," said Kurila.

Lukin hunkered down for a better look. Indeed, someone had been chopping firewood here. The chips had been trampled into the sandy dirt. "Look at the size of the chips," he said. "What does it look like they were cutting?"

Kurila picked one up and turned it over in his hand. "Maybe they had arm-sized driftwood trunks and they cut them up for a fire."

Behind them, the boatmen were bringing up cut poles for the large awning that would serve as both store and sleeping area. It would be covered over with the tarpaulins that had been wrapped around the merchandise for the journey upriver.

"How old do you think they are?" Lukin asked. He knew perfectly well, but he wanted to see if the lad could work it out for himself. The chips were still mostly bright, but had grayed a little around the edges with streaks running up the grain of the fresh faces.

Kurila scrunched up his face, thinking. "Well, they've been out in the rain for a bit."

"When's the last time it rained here?"

"Who knows? We could ask someone I guess."

"Look at the ground again. Where you picked up that chip in your hand."

The sunlit impression in the dirt where Kurila had lifted the woodchip was still dark with dampness.

"See how it's still wet underneath?" Lukin said. "If the chip had been sitting here a long time, the earth beneath it would have dried out. And the edges of the impressions would have pulled away from these other chips." He flipped over a second chip, then a third. All had damp patches beneath them, despite the dry topside of the soil facing the sky. "I'd say these have been sitting here for four or five days, maybe a bit longer, and that it rained about two days ago judging from how wet the undersides are, and the fact that the edges of the impressions haven't dried enough to truly pull away."

Kurila's eyes were solemn. "What does that tell us?"

"It tells us that the British were here already, that they stayed about a week, judging from how much firewood was cut here, and that it rained a couple days after they left."

"But Captain."

"Yes?"

"Couldn't we just find that out by asking anyone here?"

"True enough. But people don't always tell you the truth. So it's best to be able to verify what they say based on the evidence you see with your eyes. And more often than not there isn't anybody to ask."

When Kurila went off for wood Lukin stayed hunkered by the firepit, studying things. The British had come and gone already, not that that was news. Apparently it happened every summer. But if the Hudson Bay men were getting there first and buying up all the best of the lucrative sable furs, the obvious solution was to find their headquarters and evict them back over the 141st

meridian, wherever that was. Naturally this was easier said than done—Sinateh and his people were not going to be happy to see their favorite traders pushed out, and that in turn might just spark a war that could have international consequences. When Lukin left to push upriver he would be moving into the blank space that separated the two mightiest empires on the planet, and this was by no means lost on him.

Captain Lukin rose and studied the Kwifpak. Judging from the marks on the ground where the Canadian boatmen had slept he reckoned their party at eight men, maybe ten. For years the Dinneh tribes had claimed that the British were making preparations to come downriver with cannons and boats full of fighting men to destroy Nulato, and that they themselves might just join in the fun, but nothing ever seemed to come of it. As a professional fur trader, Lukin was still inclined to think this was all just fabrication calculated to play the Russian America Company off against the Hudson Bay men.

Then again, maybe it wasn't.

* * *

That night there was a dance to celebrate the arrival of the Russian traders, not that folks needed much of an excuse. The dancers from each nation—Quarrelers, Denakeh, and Tananah—mustered themselves into groups, checking each other's hair and clothing and their own faces with palm-sized looking-glasses that flashed in the sun as they were passed from hand to hand. The Tananah were the smallest troupe, even with virtually every man and woman ready and eager to step.

The dancers painted themselves with vermilion, charcoal, and yellow ochre. Many of the men danced bare-chested with every inch of exposed skin painted, even their fingers and the backs of their hands. Long strings of blue, white, and green beads with white dentalia bounced round their necks as each group moved in twin circles, one inside the other with the drummer swaying to the beat in the very center as he beat out the tempo and sang.

Sinateh was the upriver drummer. He wore so many beads and ornaments that Lukin marveled he could move under the weight of it all. The pintail feathers in his nose waggled as he sang and the dancers moved in their circles, swaying and stomping in fluid patterns that mimicked the movements of birds and the animals of the forest. They chanted in unison along with their drummer. Frequently, one or another dancer would loose a bird call, and to Lukin's eye those dancers momentarily changed into the creatures they imitated. The raw spectacle and beauty of it made his breath catch in his throat.

Larion did not drum for the Denakeh people. By his own free admission he possessed not a jot of musical talent. But he danced with his clan, whooping and moving with the whole encampment as they formed into their circles. Lukin knew the dance—the song had been composed by a second cousin of his and spoke of the music of small creeks and the blue sky reflected over their ripples. He wanted very much to join in, and then as if reading his throughs, which perhaps they had, two of the dancers broke the circle and waved him in. Lukin felt the drumbeat flowing through him in multiple directions as he moved his feet and twisted his body to the rhythm. The beat and the music and the singing beneath the endless boreal sky changed the dancers into animals, into birds and fish and spirits, and into spirit itself. Then you blinked your eyes and it was just people dancing and singing and having a good time.

The dance carried on as the sun rolled behind the tops of the spruce trees on the north bank, then angled back up again. Clocks were meaningless. There was only food and dance and fire and forest and river. In the wee hours of the morning as folks were drifting off to their beds, a girl woke Lukin trying to slip into his blankets. He'd been just falling asleep and it was the pinprick of a spruce needle poking against his neck that opened his eyes.

Zia looked down at him with the most impish of grins. She was close and naked and moving up and down against him in his clothes.

"What are you doing?" he said.

"I'm taking what's mine."

"Go away." He had no idea how she'd made it though the camp without being seen. Then again, her magic was something to be reckoned with.

"Hush," she said, grinding against him.

"I said go away."

She stopped as if slapped, then frowned and crawled out of the blankets with barely a backward glance. Nobody seemed to notice her as she walked back into the water, but then most everybody was asleep.

* * *

Trading commenced the following day after everyone had risen and shaken off the previous day's exertions. Lukin, Denisov, and Sava set out their wares on tarps spread over the ground. The Kwifpak trade, by virtue of the distance and effort involved, tended to focus on the staple items that were universally desired: knives, axes, files, needles, beads, paint, cooking pots and the like. The Company had only just the previous year approved the sale of guns to the Interior tribes, a reversal of a policy that had stood for sixty years. Any fool could see the Dinneh were buying guns in quantity from the British, and the Russian America Company needed to sell the same merchandise if they were going to stay competitive. Tailor-made clothing was not a big seller, and was not carried upriver. The Dinneh, to a man, considered their own clothing of soft leather and fur to be far superior.

Tathyaldin came first. "What do you think the hot item will be this year?" Sava asked as the Tananah chief approached with four retainers, each carrying large strings of cured pelts.

"Same as always," Lukin said. "Blue beads and ammunition."

"These guns we're selling are shit." It was true. The Company had simply sent them a shipment of whatever used firearms could be procured in St. Petersburg. Most of them were old military flintlocks refitted with lighter civilian-grade stocks. There was no telling how straight their barrels would shoot.

"I guess that's for them to figure out," Lukin said. "The beads are good quality, though."

Tathyaldin nodded a greeting to them as he ducked beneath their makeshift awning. He squatted easily on his haunches next to the arrayed merchandise, his feet flat on the ground and his knees up around his shoulders. His carriers did likewise. Lukin, Sava, and Denisov sat cross-legged across from them.

"Before we begin," Denisov said with Lukin translating into Denakeh, "we have a few small gifts for you, our valued partners in commerce." He passed over a bundle wrapped in a stack of colored kerchiefs. Tathyaldin set it on the ground before him and unrolled it. Inside were the usual items—clay pipes, tobacco, packets of needles, chunks of vermilion.

"Thank you," Tathyaldin said in Denakeh. "I have something for you as well. Call it a token of friendship." He reached into a large sack and withdrew a bundle of snow-white ermine pelts, tied together through the eyeholes with a leather thong. These he passed over to Denisov. "For your wives. Ladies love weasel pelts almost as much as flowers."

"Thank you," said Denisov. "These are very good quality. Will you have a smoke while we talk business?"

Tathyaldin reached for the new clay pipes and passed them around to his men, along with twists of the tobacco. Everyone loaded their bowls in silence, then Lukin handed over a box of matches.

"I don't know what these are," said one of the retainers, a man with the shoulders and sleeves of his shirt painted in red and gray stripes.

"Matches," Lukin said in Russian. He knew of no Denakeh word for them.

They peered over Tathyaldin's shoulder as he examined the box. Nobody seemed to know what to do with it. He shook the box, then pushed it open with his index finger.

"Like that," Lukin said, indicating Sava who was just lighting up. Their eyes slid over as Sava withdrew a match from his own box and struck it on a stone near his knee. The Tananah men's eyes went wide as the sulfur flared, then Sava lifted it to his pipe and drew the flame in long puffs. When he'd got his tobacco going, he blew out the match and tossed it aside.

Tathyaldin reached into the box and withdrew his own match. It took him three tries to get it to light. Lukin wondered if he would be startled and drop it when it finally caught—he himself had done this very thing the first time he'd struck a match—but the man coolly raised the flame to his pipe and lit it, then passed the box to the others so they might do the same.

They got down to trading right after the initial smoke. The bargaining was a slow agonizing process. Tathyaldin had plenty of fur to sell; he collected it from his various kinsmen and friends, as well as from his own traps, and in return it was his job to negotiate the best price, then distribute the proceeds accordingly.

As Lukin predicted, they wanted beads and ammunition, plus guns, naturally. All three captains had dealt with Dinneh people long enough to know what their priorities were. But there came a sticking point when Tathyaldin examined their hodgepodge inventory of used muskets and rifles. The asking price was twenty-five sable skins apiece.

"We will buy powder and lead from you," he told them, "but your guns are nowhere near as good as what the British sell." He pointed behind the Creoles to where their own guns were leaning against a log, British-made weapons with brass fittings and oversized triggerguards. "I notice you are all armed with British muskets, not Russian ones."

The captains glanced at one another. The discrepancy was obvious, but there wasn't much they could do about it.

"That's a long trip for you to travel to Fort Youcon to buy British guns," Lukin said.

"We can buy used guns from the Kutchin. They always have some for sale."

"Kutchin?" said Lukin. "I don't know that name."

"It's what the Hudson Bay men call them. I've heard you call them *Quarrelers*." He used the Russian word, translated from the original description in English from the explorer Mackenzie who'd first encountered them.

"Sinateh's people," Denisov said to Lukin, having heard the name. "The upriver Dinneh."

"These guns are also firelocks," Tathyaldin said. For these he used the English word as he pointed to the Russian weapons. "The British and the Kutchin have caplock guns like yours that always fire properly. We won't pay you twenty-five sables for any of these."

"Make us an offer," Denisov said through Lukin.

"We could pay you ten sables for a firelock gun."

Denisov shook his head. "That will not work for us," he said as Lukin translated. "These guns have to be shipped all the way around the world from St. Petersburg. That costs us very dear." He stroked his chin. "But we could take twenty for a gun."

Tathyaldin just arched an eyebrow at him.

"Will that be acceptable?" Lukin asked.

"No. We will pay no more than twelve. Take it or leave it."

Lukin pursed his lips. The Company could probably break even at fifteen sables per weapon, depending on fur prices in Moscow and Peking. Clearly, though, Tathyaldin and his men wanted guns.

* * *

Lying awake in the night on the sandy bank of the Kwifpak, Ivan Lukin tried for perhaps the ten thousandth time to imagine his father as a young man. Semyon Lukin had been a boy of seven in the year 1805 when the Kolosh took him, but he almost never talked about it. From what Zia had shown him, it was plain enough that the trauma was too much for mere words. Lukin and his siblings knew the story more as something that had always been part of their consciousness, a legacy as basic as the shape of their noses and the color of their eyes. Two years later, a passing Yankee ship captain called into the Kolosh village and bought the nine-year-old slave for three American rifles, then transported him to New Archangel and delivered him as a refugee to Aleksander Baranov, the colony's first governor. The governor took a liking to young Semyon and gave him a room in his fine two-story palace built of spruce logs. He taught him reading and writing, mathematics, geography, and of course, mercantile trade.

Even when the Imperial Navy removed Baranov from power at the direct order of the Czar for his abuses against the Native people, Semyon had nothing but praise for the man, something his son Ivan Lukin found utterly baffling.

Do we ever really know our parents? he thought somewhere in the sodden haze of insomnia. Closing his eyes in the vain quest for sleep he could see Dmitri, Anastasia, Ilya, all his own children, looking up at him. The things they outgrew and the fact that they all grew up before he was ready for them to do so, even Dmitri who was forever five years old. Semyon Lukin had shrunk a bit in his final years, stooped over from age and arthritis brought on by a lifetime of difficult travel in hard country. Toward the end, Ivan Lukin had to look down to see into his remaining eye. His mother had died while he was away at school, and he had no memories of her that weren't from the perspective of looking upward.

He must have drifted off because Sava was shaking him awake.

"What is it?" Lukin mumbled. The light had shifted toward morning. A thrush called from somewhere in the willows.

Denisov was down on one knee next to him. "You better come see this, Ivan."

He pushed himself up from his blankets and almost toppled over from lack of sleep. It felt like he was walking underwater as Denisov led him down to the beach where a crowd of early risers had gathered. They parted to reveal Sava standing over a dead man. Lukin saw straight off that he was a Russian, which was cause for concern, but as they drew nigh he saw that it was Lavrov.

"Shit," said Lukin.

Denisov squatted down next to the body and felt for a pulse, though it was plain enough the man was dead. His face was a mass of purple welts and was frozen into a grimace of excruciating pain.

"Can you ask them what happened?" Denisov asked Lukin. When Lukin voiced the question in Denakeh it seemed at first that nobody wanted to respond.

"Nobody knows?" Lukin said to the crowd.

Finally, a girl spoke up. "There is a lady down at Nowikaket under Tathyaldin's protection. This man tried to force himself into her."

Lukin translated this for Denisov and Sava. Sava pursed his lips and Denisov's face darkened noticeably. Lavrov's hands and forearms were also covered with the welts.

"They look like beestings," Lukin said.

When Sava pushed up Lavrov's sleeve there were still more welts. A yellowjacket crawled out from under his collar and sat there on the fabric for a moment. Its face was a yellow and black helmet with stubby antennae waving to and fro. Its striped abdomen pumped in and out with its breath. Above his head, Lukin heard buzzing. Another yellowjacket landed on his shoulder, then flew off in the direction of Tathyaldin's camp.

4

VANISHED IN THE NIGHT — LARION'S WARNING — THE RUSE REVEALED — SPECULATIONS — A SECOND DEPARTURE — FIRST ENCOUNTER — ATROCITY — OLD IVAN — SHOOTING LESSON — HALF THE MAN — ZIA AGAIN — AN OFFER OF HELP — AN UNHAPPY STORY — ANA RUNS — I AM NOT OF YOUR GOD — WATER HAS MEMORY — TOILING UPRIVER — THE PLEASURE OF NEW COUNTRY — GETTING CLOSE

It was customary for the fair at Nuklukayet to break up after the Russians had sold the last of their merchandise. The fireweed was just putting out its first buds, and with nothing more to purchase, there was no reason to stick around. Sinateh pulled out first, with the Quarrelers following family by family in their canoes until there were no more. The next morning the remainder of the camp woke to find that Tathyaldin and his people had vanished during the night, every man, woman, and child. Presumably they were headed back to their mountains. Lavrov's death already had Larion on edge, but the shaman's sudden and silent departure had him visibly rattled. He and his own people struck their camps and set off downriver that very afternoon.

"Little Cousin," he said to Lukin as his wives were loading the family's canoes, "you and your friends would be wise to come with us."

"Why is that?" Lukin seriously doubted that Denisov would consent to traveling downriver with Larion. Indeed, he'd told Lukin the wisest strategy was to make sure you departed before he did and row like hell downstream so as to minimize the potential for an ambush.

"Tathyaldin is not to be trusted. I think he is planning something." A noise in the trees caught Larion's attention. He cocked an ear to listen, then saw it was only a robin rustling in the leaves on the forest floor.

"I think we'll stay another day or two," Lukin said.

Larion's eyes were flat and hard as he scanned the edge of the forest and the hills beyond.

"The Company wants us to scout timber for a new fort here."

"You may pay a steep price for it," Larion cautioned. "Tathyaldin has the power to make himself invisible, which is deadly in an ambush."

Lukin smiled. "I've heard he can only make himself invisible when nobody's looking."

"This is no joking matter, Little Cousin. You saw your dead countryman just as I did. Those yellowjackets are his magic at work."

"Do you know for certain he is planning something?"

"I have reason to suspect. Come downriver with us. There is safety in numbers."

Lukin thought to comment that Larion had not exactly shown himself to be trustworthy over the years but decided against it. "We are servants of the Company. We do what they require of us."

"Those half-Kolosh fools are no concern of yours."

"Actually, they are. The three of us go way back."

"Have it your way," Larion said, shaking his head. Two of his family's canoes were already pushing off. He walked to the remaining boat and pushed it into the shallows with his oldest wife and their son and they all hopped in. Sitting in the stern, Larion raised a hand, then pushed into the current with his paddle.

In a matter of hours the Russians were the only souls left at Nuklukayet. This was a specific relief, actually, given that Lukin's journey was only just beginning. There had been a worry that folks would linger as the fair broke up and then start asking questions as to why the Russians hadn't left yet, and more to the point why Lukin was suddenly building a canoe. That same afternoon he set about peeling birchbark and splitting out frame pieces.

"This place is damned lonely without everyone here," Sava said that night around their fire. Indeed, the camping ground seemed a vast empty space behind them.

"I'm impressed you got Tathyaldin to leave so quickly," Denisov said to Lukin.

"All it took was some cheap flintlock guns." Lukin had in fact struck a bargain with the Tananah chieftain whereby he could have all the unsold guns for free if he and his people vacated in the middle of the night so as to cause a stir the following day. Tathyaldin had been delighted at the prospect, both for the sake of acquiring the guns and because he loathed Larion and relished the opportunity to get under his skin.

"Larion took off like his hair was on fire," Sava commented.

"I think that's all the evidence one needs of how much influence Tathyaldin wields hereabouts," Lukin replied. "He's the man we need on our side if the Company's going to be pushing up the Tananah River."

After a while, Sava asked, "Do you think the Company really is going to build a new for here?"

"They might," Denisov said. "Once we deal with the British and get control of the upriver trade."

"If we could capture the commerce on the Tananah we could maybe use it as a wedge to force them out," Lukin mused. Being the tip of the spear on such an important operation was intoxicating. His father had built the Company's commerce on the Kuskokwim from the ground up and it seemed obvious that he could be the man to do the same on the Tananah.

"We'll have a ready-built fort up the Kwifpak," Sava said. "All we have to do is get the Hudson Bay men out. Then between Fort Youcon and Nuklukayet we'd command the whole Interior."

"If the British don't burn the fort to the ground when they leave," Denisov said in a dour voice.

Lukin munched on a rusk, mulling over the possibilities.

"What will you do if they recognize you at Fort Youcon?" Kurila asked him.

Denisov paused in the middle of lighting his pipe, watching.

"Sinateh himself might discover you," Sava said. "I never considered that."

Lukin yawned again, feeling the sawdust in his eyes and the tug of sleep. Tired as he was now from a night and a day without sleep, he knew that as soon as he lay down he would be wide awake and unable to escape his daytime mind. He held on to a vague hope that lining a canoe upriver for a few weeks would render him so bone-weary at the end of each day that he would just collapse into unconsciousness.

"I'll just have to trust God's plan and go over the side of that bridge in flames when I get to it."

* * *

The three trading boats departed two days later when Lukin had completed his canoe. They shook hands, bade each other farewell, and Lukin stood alone on the beach watching the flotilla stroke out into the river as the current took hold and started pulling them back to Nulato. Denisov had put Yarko the Finlander at the helm of Lukin's boat. He hoped the man would not go too hard on Kurila.

Sava turned at the tiller. "Until later, Ivan!"

Denisov raised a hand in salute, and to Lukin's surprise, so did several of the crew. He returned the wave and watched as the three boats vanished around the bend, one after another, and was somewhat envious of their downstream ease. With the demise of Lavrov, the Finlander's new command was missing an oarsman, but oar strength was less important when you were going with the flow.

Lukin watched downriver, noticing the moon sliding down behind the trees in the summer sunlight. His heart ached for Ilya and Anastasia; missing your family was always a dull weight you dragged behind you, yet the weight seemed to slip effortlessly between the trees of the forest as you walked. He was aware that he should feel something for Iriana, but he couldn't find anything. For all he knew she had taken a lover to warm the bed in his absence.

It was not so much duty to the Company or the desire to repair his good name that compelled him to put his new canoe in the water, but the empty loneliness of Nuklukayet abandoned. He let out a long sigh and listened to the song of a sparrow somewhere in the willows nearby. Then he pushed off from shore, headed into the no-man's land between empires. The moon had disappeared, but she would be back for him.

* * *

It was the term break before Lukin's final year of school in New Archangel when he first encountered Zia. The vast distances across Russian America dictated that hardly any students got to go home between trimesters, so young Lukin mostly ran wild in the rainforest around the town while being nominally looked after by a family of Yosif Denisov's local relatives. He had not seen his home for four years. In his mind he was more a castaway than a scholar.

There was a little cove he'd discovered earlier in the spring. Just a minor indentation in the outside coast with rocky headlands and a sandy beach where a stream tumbled down from the mountains. Drift logs lay jumbled up like a retaining wall between the grass and the beach flowers and the damp ocean sand below. He had lately taken to going barefoot and shirtless in the forest like the Kolosh did, with the legs of his broadfall sailcloth trousers turned up to the calf. He followed a deer path through the grass and over the logs to the sand where he squatted down and watched the water, the gray sky, the line where they came together.

There was the slightest of noises to his left and he turned to see one of the logs moving. He stood up sharply, his pulse jumping. It was impossible not to hear the tales of Kolosh shamans who could change themselves into rocks or trees or what have you, but he'd never seen such a thing himself. Until now.

He blinked at the upright figure. He had expected some wretchedly ugly old man, or perhaps a wizened crone with one eye gone milky and breasts that hung to her navel. The figure was indeed female and naked, but came in the form of a girl, a scant year or two older than him. She had smallish breasts and the beginnings of a dark pubic triangle.

Young Lukin stood still as a rock, watching her eyes as she studied him. Inside there formed a williwaw of emotion, a mix of body shame learned from the priests, with the memory of aunts, uncles, and cousins back home who shed their clothes in public when taken by the notion to do so, more or less without a second thought. And beneath that was something far more basic than emotion or wonder. It came in the sensation of sun-warmed planks on the soles of his feet, a flush in parts of him that he'd not been aware of before, not the least inside his trousers.

Her most noticeable feature, beyond her nakedness, was the snarl of matted hair that crowned her head and trailed down onto the ground behind her.

"Who are you?" she said in Russian.

"Who are you?" Lukin returned.

"I asked you first."

"Ivan Semyonovich Lukin. I go to school in town."

She had not moved an inch since standing up. "You've been here before."

He felt a wash of embarrassment. He'd never told anyone about this cove; it was a place he ran to when life in New Archangel became too overwhelming, which was often enough.

"I've watched you," she said. "You come here a lot."

"It's quiet here. Do you live in town?"

She shook her head. "I live here."

"But you speak Russian."

"My father was Russian."

"What about your mother?"

"She was Tlingit. You call us Kolosh."

"So you're Creole."

Her mouth twitched into something close to a smile. “That’s what the people in town would call me.”

Lukin was feeling restless, thinking he should say something else, something of greater import than establishing that she was a Creole. “Do you have a house out here?”

“Sort of. Are you hungry?”

"I guess."

She hopped down from the drift logs into the packed beach. Her bare feet landed on a patch of gravel but if it hurt she gave no indication. "Come on," she said, walking toward the ocean.

"I don't know your name," Lukin called after her.

"Zia." Her ankles were already splashing into the water. Lukin could only follow.

He stopped to roll his pantlegs up higher. Zia was soon up to her waist, the long felty ropes of her hair floating behind her. Lukin waded gingerly among the barnacles and mussels embedded in the gravel. It was hard to see where he was stepping for the seaweed and kelp strings that furled gently in the small shore waves. The water was very cold, but then he’d swum and played in cold water his entire life.

He set his foot down on something squishy and yanked it back up again. It turned out to be a sun star, an oversized starfish with a dozen or more arms extending from a disc-like central body. Young Lukin jumped sideways, sloshing wildly in the shallows.

"He won't hurt you," Zia called. "I've known him for years. He's friendly."

He regained both his balance and a measure of composure. He had the distinct impression Zia was laughing at him, though her face was turned down to peer at the seafloor with her face hidden inside the mass of her hair.

She drew a deep breath, then to Lukin's surprise plunged into the water. Nothing remained but a ring of ripples and roiling water, and all he could do was wait for her to surface and try not to feel like a helpless fool.

She surfaced several yards out in the cove and side-stroked until she could stand in the shallows again. When she regained her feet the ocean sluiced over her breasts and her nipples stood out like tree stumps. Lukin was aware of how hard he had suddenly become, despite the icy water. Reflexively he hunched in on himself to try and hide the erection and for a moment he thought he might faint. Then Zia held up four good-sized tanner crabs, two in each hand by their hind legs. Their free limbs waved slowly in the air as she waded back to shore.

"Howcome you didn't come any further out?" she asked.

"It's cold."

Zia nodded gravely at this as she splashed up onto the sand. She set the crabs on their backs to prevent their escape, then sat with her knees drawn up to her chest. It offered an intriguing view of her legs and it was all Lukin could do not to stare. At least he knew how to light a fire; he began gathering up the makings from the driftwood above the wrack line.

"How'd you get all those crabs?" he finally asked, dumping the sticks onto the sand. He drew his flint, steel, and tinderbox from his pocket, then took a knee and struck a spark onto some charcoal in the tin. This he plucked up and set into a nest of dried grass and blew until it blazed into flame.

"Easy," she said. "After the summer solstice when the moon is full they come up into the bays and coves. You can pick them up with your hands."

The wood was dry enough to burn, but still a tad damp. It sent up billows of steam with the smoke. Lukin looked up at the overcast sky. The gray clouds had the look of a soggy blanket. “How can you tell the moon is full? It's been cloudy for days and days."

"Women always know."

He drew his pipe and tobacco from his other pocket.

"You got tobacco?" Zia's eyes lit up, which made him smile.

"I do. You have a pipe?"

She lifted a hank of her matted hair and withdrew a stubby soapstone pipe from the tangle of felt at the back of her head, which struck Lukin as a convenient place to keep it, given the lack of pockets in her birthday suit. She blew into the bowl to dry it out, then accepted the tin Lukin offered and filled up. Lukin took a flaming brand from the fire and held it to the bowl as she puffed, then he lit his own.

Zia smoked with obvious pleasure, holding the smoke in for several seconds before blowing it back out. "We should cook them now. It's going to rain again."

Lukin pushed his knife into each crab's brain while Zia used a stick to rake the coals into a bed. Then she laid each crab onto the coals and scraped more over their backs. They had another smoke while their supper steamed inside the shell, then they pulled them from the fire and broke them open to eat the cooked flesh with their fingers.

Lukin was just licking his fingers when he felt the cold pinprick of a raindrop on the back of his hand. It was followed by another, then two more, then the whole sky opened up. Raindrops hissed in the coals and quickly darkened the sand.

"Told you," Zia said, reaching behind her head to tuck her pipe back into its home. It came to Lukin in that moment that she did not have the slit lip you would expect to see on a Kolosh woman who had come of age.

She stood. "Come on. I want to show you something."

Lukin rose as the rain intensified. She led him across the darkening sand to where the creek tumbled down a series of rocky chutes choked with devils club and fallen trees to a lagoon that was filling with seawater from the incoming tide. She beckoned Lukin back into the water and waded across the mouth to the far side where it pooled up against a rocky overhang. Here the water was ever so slightly sheltered from the rain and the surface was calm. The mixing of salt and fresh water made a disorienting swirl inside the structure of the liquid. The dim shapes of coho salmon milled about.

"What did you want to show me?" Lukin asked.

Zia giggled a little. Standing next to him in the water she spread her palms out over the surface and slid them apart. The surface shimmered ever so slightly and there was a village of sod houses on a treeless shore.

"What is this?" he asked.

"An island. You call it Kadyak."

There were a dozen men. He recognized many of them as Cossacks by their shaved heads and long mustaches. A minority of the men were Russians. Their bidarkas pulled up on the beach. One of the Cossacks was filing up a dozen or so old men and women, some of whom hobbled along on crutches and sticks of driftwood. He directed them to stand back to front, hugging the person before them. Their clothes were of birdskin and otter and seal pelts. A couple of the old men wore hats made of steambent planks adorned with the whiskers of sea otters. None of them seemed to have any idea what was happening.

The Cossack stepped back and gave a signal. A Russian came up with a musket, knelt in front of the grandmother at the front of the line. He cocked the flint, took a bead so that the muzzle was inches away from her belly.

"No," whispered Lukin. Zia said nothing. He was vaguely aware that she was watching him instead of the water.

The man squeezed the trigger and the musket cracked the air. The grandmother blinked, then her eyes opened wide, then she blinked again and staggered sideways. The man behind her crumpled, clutching his abdomen, and the old woman behind him let out a moan that rose gradually into a scream. Those behind her were unpunctured but stood in shocked disbelief as the Russians and Cossacks burst out in laughter. The Cossack who had stood them together came up and clapped the gunman on the shoulder. The wind broke up the cloud of sulfur gunsmoke and carried it across the bay as those gutshot by the bullet writhed in the dead grass and melting snow and those unhurt crouched and crawled over to comfort them. One of the old men wearing a bentwood hat grabbed a beach rock and fired it from his hand at the head of the Cossack with an arm trained from fifty years of aiming spears. It struck him square on the temple and he dropped to the beach. The old hunter had a second rock for the gunman but a shot from another musket punched through his chest. He staggered, then loosed the missile and it grazed the head of the gunman who was frantically reloading his musket, then another red blossom opened on his center and his sealgut raincoat belled out behind him in a spray of red. He crumpled over, then fell as the wails rose from the beach again. The old man pushed himself up on knees, gripping another rock, but the gunman walked fast up to him and shoved the barrel of his musket against his head and blew his brains onto the grass.

"Why?" young Lukin whispered. "Why are you showing me this?"

Zia reached out and pushed a lock of his hair behind his ear. "He looks like you."

And indeed he did. The Russian gunman reloaded his piece as the village elders moaned and tried to help the wounded. The more Lukin looked the more he saw the man had his same jawline and nose. That his beard grew heavy on his upper lip, just as Semyon's had. Lukin always been told that he looked like his Russian grandfather, a man he'd only ever heard called Old Ivan. And now here he was.

Another Russian shouted a command and a string of six prisoners was led down onto the beach. All were young women. Old Ivan threw his musket over his shoulder and straightened his powderhorn and shotpouch under his arm and ambled down to where they were brought to a halt. The men were examining them, feeling them up like livestock. Old Ivan stopped at the penultimate girl in the line and gave her a thorough appraisal with his free hand. She tried to bite his thumb off when he gripped her cheeks to tilt her face toward him. I think you will be my wife, he said to her. Your name is Ana.

Over the rush of the cataract there came a shout, muffled by the evergreen forest around them. Lukin squinted through the rain across the tide lagoon to see a figure standing under the shelter of a Kolosh spruceroot hat. It was Yosif Denisov.

"Get away from her, Ivan!" he shouted at Lukin, pointing.

"What?"

Denisov took up a stick of driftwood and hurled it at Zia. She reached out and caught it, inches from her head. She hissed a Kolosh curse and slung it back at him.

"*Move!*" Yosif bellowed as he ducked the stick. Lukin glanced back down at the water where the image of Old Ivan dissipated into the shape of a coho. Denisov flung a rock at Zia and she caught that too. Lukin inched away, lost his balance and tumbled into the water, then bolted away from her. When he looked back, Zia had changed herself into a river otter, still watching him. Above the sky the clouds had begun to tear apart in some high-up wind. They raced out to sea with their jagged edges peeling away to nothingness as the rain slackened, then disappeared.

"What are you doing here?" Denisov asked when Lukin got back down to the beach.

"I come out here sometimes to have a smoke. Watch the ocean and get away from folks."

"You shouldn't be out here," Denisov said as he kept a wary eye on the otter that was suddenly floating in the pool, watching them.

"Why not?"

"That girl is dangerous."

"What are you talking about?"

Denisov looked around, then leaned into Lukin and whispered a word in his ear. "She's the ghost of someone's cousin who drowned. She'll take you into the water and make you join her. Eat your soul."

Later that night in the rare clear sky, Lukin noted that it was a waxing quarter moon. Scored upon its face like lines carved in a cedar plank was the image of a beast, teeth bared and watching him. He watched this icon graven onto the moon as it floated above the cedar shake roofs, wishing despite his better judgment for another vision of his family's past.

* * *

Traveling alone on the Kwifpak, he carried three musket balls tucked into the space between fingers of his left hand, even when he slept. The Koltsan hunter who'd shown him the handful of golden bullets years before had impressed upon him the importance of always having ammunition literally in your hand at all times for emergencies. He'd also taught Lukin how to reload and fire a musket in a matter of seconds by pouring in the gunpowder then slipping a ball into the barrel with no wadding, then slamming the butt against the ground to drive it home. The lack of wadding meant your bullet wouldn't fly very true, but then as the hunter had told Lukin, you didn't need to hit a hundred-yard mark dead-on when you were being chased through the woods. You just needed to hit the man ten feet away who was chasing you with an axe.

He carried a light traveling kit—blankets and a tarp, a kettle, an axe. His musket and a small cask of rusks. Another of dried fish. Also some roasted moose meat he'd bartered from one of Sinateh's cousins. His battered copy of *The Synaxarion*, detailing the lives of the Orthodox saints. The old shirt he'd bought from one of Tathyaldin's hunters for a brass teapot. All together it wasn't much weight, and he knew how to build a canoe so it sat light in the water with a minimum of drag for paddling and poling.

All the same it was much slower going as a single paddler in a canoe. He only made ten miles that first day. He'd been craving a little solitude, but there was no question that it was a lot nicer to be the captain in the stern of a boat with six oarsmen to do the rowing. There was plenty of time to listen to the sound of the river, but it wasn't necessarily so pleasant when that sound included your legs sloshing through the shallows as you dragged your boat upstream.

He stared into his evening fire, thinking of something Denisov had said to him the night before they left on the return to Nulato. The conversation around the captains' fire had turned back to the Fort Kolmakov Incident, as folks were evidently calling it now. "I heard Metrikov say you weren't half the man your father was," Denisov had said quietly, something for which Lukin had no answer but cold impotent rage.

"Half the man indeed," he said to the coals of his solitary fire. Sergei Metrikov knew nothing of who his father had been. Lukin was forced to wonder how much longer he could go without smacking the Nulato bidarshik, and action that seemed unwise given the fact that he outweighed Lukin by a good forty pounds, in addition to outranking him. Lazy clouds drifted across the cerulean blue of the night sky and he watched the etchings in the face of the quarter moon as it pushed up behind the rumpled trunks of the cottonwood trees.

* * *

He woke that night to something poking his ribs. He rolled over and saw her kneeling in the shallows of the water with her long felt-like locks trailing in the current behind her, smiling as she held the other end of a long willow wand.

"You haven't aged a day, Zia."

She giggled.

Lukin frowned and sat up. There was some mild resentment at the fact that he'd actually been fast asleep for once.

"I didn't wake you, did I?"

"Someone's feeling mischievous tonight." He struck a match and lit some gudge in the censer to drive the mosquitoes away, then came down and sat cross-legged next to the dark rim of sand at the water's edge.

"Come closer," Zia said.

"I don't want to get wet."

"I want to touch you again."

He just smiled at her, keeping his distance. "Let me help you. This curse that burdens you can be lifted through prayer."

Zia shook her head, then waved a palm as if wiping his words from the air. "That is not what I came to see you about."

"What then?"

"I wanted to ask about Natalia."

It felt like someone had poured a bucket of cold water down the back of his shirt. "What about her?"

"Did you love her?"

"What kind of question is that?"

"It's a very simple one."

"I suppose I did." He looked down at the water between them, how it gently slid up and down the silky youthful skin of her folded knees. He knew he needed to be honest with her. "But our marriage was arranged for us by our families. She was the granddaughter of an important Koltsan chief. It was more of a commercial transaction to cement the trade with them, but I suppose we did learn to love each other, in some ways at least."

"Is there any truth to this rumor that you shot her dead in a drunken rage?"

Lukin glared at her.

"Please don't be angry."

He took a deep breath. "It was an accident, as has been said many times before."

Zia closed her eyes. "What happened?"

"It was the year after Larion sacked Nulato and we had several loaded muskets in the house in case he came down to Kolmakov looking for trouble. One of them went off and hit her."

"Say more about that." Over the river a raven called as it flew to somewhere. Zia's eyes remained closed.

Lukin profoundly did not wish to discuss his awful memories with her, but then there seemed to be no other way to help her.

"It was when she was cooking supper," he said. "I was moving the muskets upstairs so the children couldn't get at them. My daughter Anastasia was only two at the time, just learning to walk properly." He stopped, gathering both thought and love to give himself strength.

"Go on."

"She tripped and fell next to the pitchka furnace. She put her hands out to catch herself and pushed them right onto the hot iron door."

Zia opened her eyes. "That must have hurt."

"She had horrible burns. Even now her palms and one of her forearms are a mass of scars. She started screaming like crazy and in the rush I left one of the guns on a bench where a spark from the fire escaped and landed on the touchhole. Natalia was holding her and she just happened to be in the way of the shot. It went in here," Lukin said, poking an index finger into the left side of his ribcage.

Neither of them spoke for several heartbeats. There was only the sound of the river.

"I have something to show you," Zia said.

Lukin's pulse quickened. "Show me."

The current was slightly rumpled in the small water between them, some tiny rapid, a miniature version of the bigger runs through the ramparts. Zia leaned forward and smoothed the water like sand. There were girthy cottonwood trees, summer dampness, songbirds. A creek nearby and a steep treeless hillside beyond. The blossoms of fireweed and the palmate leaves of puchki plants. Footsteps, then Ana bursting through the brush, panting, obviously terrified. She wore a rude approximation of a Russian sarafan dress and it was only when she turned to look behind her that Lukin saw the bulge of her belly. There was a bear nearby and she knew it but that was not what she was running from. A stick snapped, then a voice shouted. She turned and ran, but got tangled in a patch of head-high willows. She hunkered down, trembling, trying to hide amid the thick brush and it seemed for a moment that whatever it was would pass her by but then a hand gripped her hair and yanked her up and dragged her out of the willows as she clawed at the arm connected to it. Old Ivan, half drunk and interrupted from dark thoughts of his old life outside St. Petersburg. Indentured at the age of six to work in the sawpits cutting timber to build the Czar's navy. The clink of coins in his own father's palm as the officer in his powdered wig and tricorne hat gripped his tiny hand and pulled him bawling from his mother. Never to see them again. Sleeping huddled in the piles of sawdust after the day's work with the other boys, none older than nine or ten.

Old Ivan pulled Ana his wife from the willowbrush and out into the more open ground beneath the cottonwoods and struck her across her already bruised face. You need to be corrected, he said as the other Russians and Cossacks came running up. This behavior of yours is not acceptable. He fumbled with his breeches as the others stood around them in a circle, men with pale skin and long beards, men with darker skin and jetblack hair dressed in the clothes of strange Asian tribes she had only heard about as distant stories. She whispered out the name of the man she was married to when these Cossacks came to the village and with it went the will to resist.

"I wanted to hear it from you," Zia said.

Lukin looked up from the water. Tears had pooled in his eyes, tears of shame, of pain, an ache deep in the soul for which he could find no name. "Why must you keep following me?" he asked, dragging a sleeve across his face.

"Because I need you. And you need me. You need the things I show you. Why do you keep trying to set me free?"

"Because I love God. And all of his creatures."

She frowned, unmoved. "You know I am not of your God."

"His love is infinite. And that commands me to help you."

After she left he lay back down under his mosquito net thinking, *What am I to do with all these things that have passed?*

* * *

He made the foot of the Kwifpak ramparts after three days of lining upstream, this being a section where the river necked down into a narrow chute between high walls of bedrock filled with rapids. He was going entirely on information provided by Larion and other Natives of his acquaintance who'd traveled upriver, as well as general hearsay he'd picked up over the last twenty-odd years.

When Lukin was nine years old, a Kolosh shaman on the island of Sitkah had told him that water had a memory just like a person's, but far more vast and comprehensive. Young Lukin had seen this fellow deep in conversation with bears on two separate occasions, so he seemed like someone to pay attention to. The priests who ran the school, however, laughed at this notion and told him in no uncertain terms that it was a sin to hold such beliefs.

Even so, many years later, the idea had never left him. On his first trip up the Kuskokwim with his father, a Koltsan healer-woman had pointed at the river and told him that every drop of water carries with it the memory of every rock it has flowed over, every animal that has drunk from it. Every time it froze and thawed, and every fish that cut through its current.

"That's an awful lot to remember," Lukin had told her.

"It is," she replied. "But still, the water knows. You must always be careful how you speak of it."

He'd wondered more than once over the years as Zia kept returning whether or not she was some manifestation of water's memory. Denisov had understood her without a moment's doubt to be a malevolent spirit. But Lukin had never heard of such a creature following someone away from its country. He had no Kolosh people handy to ask other than Denisov, and he was reticent to speak on the subject. Lukin's desire was less to convert her to the faith than to simply set her spirit free. He had no answer for this.

More than once as he waded and poled up the Kwifpak he wondered if the Kuskokwim River remembered him in particular, and if it missed him the way he missed it. Native folks of his acquaintance generally regarded the idea of being removed from their country as the most terrifying of prospects. You heard stories of people kidnapped, either by neighboring tribes or by the early Russian hunters, who just folded into themselves with grief. What could you do in a foreign land where your feet didn't know the shape of the earth and the water didn't remember you?

It took him a full day to portage around the ramparts, then with his canoe back in the water the upstream work began anew. For several days after the portage there were mountains on the north bank, not too dissimilar from the rounded hills around Fort Kolmakov. A few were high enough to have bald tops and he wondered if mountain sheep could be found up there, not that he had the time to go look. He saw no high craggy peaks or glaciers as there were in the country of the Koltsan, though there were plenty of spots where the hills ran right down to the river and were cut away into steep cliffs.

The south bank was lower, swampier, a mosaic of white and black spruce. It was also considerably buggier. When ashore he worked with the omnipresent kerchief around his face and a Denakeh buckskin hood over his head with cascades of fringe around the edges. The fringes flopped and jiggled with his every movement, keeping all but the most determined mosquitoes away. He smeared grease on his face, neck, hands, and arms for extra protection, but this came at a cost: the grease made him feel hot, and the weather was already plenty warm. As much as he could, he made his camps atop the crags of the north shore. He had to haul water up from the river, but at least there was wind to snatch the bugs away. He'd brought a cake of homemade soap, but didn't use it because stink, grease, and grime together were among the very best of insect repellents.

He had dry fish to eat but made a pleasure of stopping when he could to hunt waterfowl and upland birds. Near the upper end of the hills he spied fifty or so caribou swimming across the river from the south bank, likely desperate to escape the mosquitoes. Lukin poled his canoe hard next to the bank until he was within twenty feet of a small bull. His velvet-covered antlers swung to and fro as he swam next to his herdmates. Their puffs and grunts were audible all around. The bull rolled his eyes over at Lukin as he paced him in the canoe. He was sliding downstream with the current now, but so were the deer. He waited until the bull had the bottom beneath his feet, then he took up his gun, cocked it, and waited until his bow turned upriver. The bull staggered a bit from shifting its balance from water to land, then humped up onto the bank. Lukin traced him through his sights onto the shore, and squeezed off the shot when he paused to look back. The bull sank down, hindquarters first, then rose and plowed forward several steps, then fell again, dead.

Three times in the following days he saw bears on the bank, but they did not bother him so he left them alone in kind. Daily he was astounded by how much moose sign he encountered above the ramparts: tracks in the sand, willows clipped off from feeding, hair snagged on close-hanging spruce boughs. Moose were exceedingly scarce on the lower Kwifpak; Lukin knew grown men who had never laid eyes on one. He'd been raised largely on moose meat and regarded moose backstrap dredged in flour and pan fried as the very taste of success in life, not that there had been much of that lately.

He came across Quarreler fish camps on six different occasions at the mouths of various tributaries. Each time he let himself drift back down until he was out of sight, then he crossed the river and came back up on the far side in the small hours of the morning. It would be regarded as highly unusual for a traveler on the river to not stop and say hello, but many of these folk were likely to recognize him from the trade fair and it wouldn't do for rumors of a Russian traveling alone to precede him upriver.

Gradually the mountains and cliffs on the north bank peeled away and flattened out. Now both banks were low and swampy. The river braided itself into a maze of channels and it was only Lukin's expert riverman's eye that kept him on the main course. But at least the current became sluggish enough that he could make headway with just a paddle.

And he knew he was getting close. His intelligence from people who had made the trip was that once you hit the flats it was only four or five more days to the mouth of a large clear-water tributary that ran down from the northeast. The Quarrelers he'd spoken to called it the Choonjik River. Fort Youcon, he'd been advised, was just a few hundred fathoms up from the confluence.

He paddled. He camped in the best wind he could find. He lined the canoe when he had to. He dined on dried and smoked caribou meat. And he worried day and night about how all this would go. On some nights he managed to sleep several hours in a row.

5

FORT YOUCON — SENTINEL OF THE SPRUCE FOREST — WHAT IF — A WHOLE NEW MAN —INITIATIVE — CANOES AND CANADIANS — INTO THE LION'S DEN — OBSERVATIONS — OVER THE FALLS — DISCOVERED — THE HUDSON BAY BIDARSHIK — INTERPRETATION — CARDS ON THE TABLE — UNDIGNIFIED EXIT — FIREWEED IN BLOOM

It was drizzling rain when he finally caught sight of the British fort. Following the directions, he turned up the Choonjik, then he poled up its course and kept on for another half mile or so until he came around a bend and there it was on the left bank.

There was a stockade of upright logs with a tower built at each corner. He noted right off that the British towers were built in a square pattern rather than the octagonal Russian layout he was accustomed to. Dozens of dome-shaped skin tents were clustered around the palisade; these he recognized as the lodges of the Quarrelers. On the bank in front of the fort lay several dozen canoes, along with four large plank boats, which he took to be the Hudson Bay Company's version of the Russian bidara. In the distance he could hear a dog chorus. In fact, from this far out the place didn't seem all that different from Nulato. Or Fort Kolmakov or Fort St. Michael for that matter.

Raindrops pocked the river all around his canoe and low gray clouds dragged through the low sky above. Lukin rested with his paddle across the gunwales, drifting silently and watching. He wore a kamleik for the rain; beneath it his clothes were sweaty and damp.

It seemed utterly improbable that the British could have traversed all that blank space on the maps, but here they were. He shivered a little as rainwater dripped from the bill of his corduroy cap.

"The damned Kolosh can have this shitty weather," he muttered, then dug his paddle into the water as the fort receded again behind the bend. He pointed for shore to change his clothes.

In the woods, water dripped everywhere. He knew he had to be somewhere near the Arctic Circle, for the sun had not been dipping below the northern horizon. Even Nulato was far enough south that the solstice sun would roll briefly behind the Earth, then rise a couple hours later.

The rain was actually a good thing in that it would wipe out any tracks he made on the sand of the riverbank when he beached his canoe and carried it on one shoulder up the bank and into the trees. He had to doff the kamleika lest it snag on a branch and tear. It was a perfect garment for the treeless Aleutian Islands where it had been invented, but way up here it was no good except when out on the water.

He cached his canoe well into the forest and covered it with cut boughs to camouflage it. Then he returned for his pack, keeping his feet on the wet rocks as much as possible so as to leave no tracks in the sand. Nothing in the woods moved except for a squirrel that chattered at him from atop a distant black spruce, a sharp click followed by a whiny churring until he'd passed. He could feel the pugnacious rodent's eye on him as he trudged through the spongy wet moss, each step squishing water through his moccasins and the wool stockings underneath. At least the rain would be keeping everyone around the fort close to home.

Further back among the trees he broke dry twigs from a sheltering spruce tree and made a tiny fire for tea, stuffing pieces of dried caribou meat into his mouth as the kettle hissed. This far north the forests clung to the rivers and ponds in discrete ribbons where the soil was marginally warmer. You could only go so deep in these woods before you came out the other side, and he eyed the lighter space through the trunks of birch, spruce, and cottonwood where the tall forest petered out into waist-high black spruce, and then to tussock tundra. He sugared his tea and drank it, then smoked a pipe and tried not to worry about how all this would go. There seemed to be a fair chance that somebody would recognize him. By this time tomorrow he might be tied up in one of the blockhouses awaiting extradition to Montreal. Or perhaps they would try to use him as a bargaining chip with the Russian America Company.

More or less out of nowhere, Sava's suggestion bounced into his mind—that he tell the Hudson Bay men he was a deserter from downriver. He'd been reaching for more dry meat but froze in place, so sudden was the notion. He had five hundred rubles in gold, with more to come. And his knowledge of the Russian America Company could make him a real asset to the Hudson Bay men.

He pulled his pipe from his mouth and sat for a long moment, thinking, *What if I'm the one doing the bargaining?*

* * *

Fortune favors the bold, Semyon Lukin often told his children. Sometime in the gray night Lukin woke to find the world slightly lighter than when he left it. The rain had quit but the sky was the same color as the ashes in his fire pit. He slipped down to the river to fill his kettle, then he rekindled the fire and made tea. The air itself held the feeling that today was to be an auspicious beginning. The first day of the rest of his life, as it were.

After drinking his morning tea he reached into his pack and withdrew a razor and his cake of soap. The time had come to slip over the boundary into life as a Dinneh hunter.

Back home, at Iriana's request, he always kept his beard trimmed close to the face, but over the weeks he'd been on the river it had grown out considerably. Shirtless in the damp chilly woods, he stropped the blade and shaved it off with the aid of small looking-glass. He would have fresh stubble within two days, but he only needed today for this mission. Whenever the blade wasn't against his face he sang old Deghitan songs from his childhood. The shave took close to an hour. When he was done he thought about having more tea, but decided to just get things moving. The squirrels had gone quiet for the time being, and the rattle of a woodpecker drilling into a dead tree somewhere drifted through the morning. He talked softly to the woodpecker in Koltsan.

Lukin set his cloth clothes aside and slipped the old Tananah shirt over his head. It had been tailored from skins of young caribou killed in the early summer and it hung big and loose on his frame. The inside of the neck was dark and greasy from grime, sweat, and grease accumulated in a hunter's life, but that was so much the better for his disguise.

He found his grease tin and scooped out a large lump with his fingertips. This he rubbed all over his face and hair, his hands and forearms. It was the standard measure against the bugs, but the Quarrelers like most of the Dinneh considered it a mark of beauty and status to have a good coat of grease on your skin at all times. It showed you to be a skilled and active hunter, or the wife or child of one. Lukin took a little extra grease and mixed it in his palm with vermilion powder to make a red paint that he smeared with his fingers into a mask that covered his forehead, his eyelids, the bridge of his nose and the tops of his cheekbones. He pulled his long hair from its braid, carefully combing it out, then he ran his red fingers through his locks to make greasy red streaks. The front half of his hair he let hang loose to better disguise his face; the back half he pulled into a long tail that he wrapped closely with a string of blue beads.

When it was all done he studied his disguise in the looking-glass. It would get him in the front gate, he reckoned. He was still working up the courage to make the next move, but the immediate task was to scout things out.

* * *

It took him nearly an hour to creep around to the north side of the fort, moving through the wet forest and keeping to the dense brush as much as he could to avoid being seen. Despite his best efforts, his pants and the pointed tails of his shirt were soaked and the wet leather was clammy against his thighs as he stood just inside the edge of the timber, watching. The stump field surrounding the fort was laced with footpaths from the comings and goings of the residents.

"Here I go," he whispered, stepping out from the forest and onto a well-trod path that angled in from the river. Down at the waterfront he noticed that several of the Hudson Bay canoes were as long as a bidara and were built in a curious configuration he'd never encountered: round bottoms and ends that swept up into high graceful curves at the bow and stern. Two men—Canadians he surmised, judging from their dark complexions and the French they seemed to be speaking—were caulking the seams of one of these leviathan craft. Lukin recognized the language from back at New Archangel where many of the priests educated in Russia spoke it among themselves. One raised a hand and called out a greeting. Lukin returned the gesture and kept moving, following the trail through the stumps as it veered toward a broader path that appeared to lead to the fort's main gate. It was strewn with woodchips and crisscrossed with the shallow roots of dead spruce trees.

Most of the Quarreler tents stood off to his right, downriver of the fort on the south-facing side where they would catch the most sunlight. Drying racks stood everywhere, festooned with meat and split fish fillets joined at the tails. Now he could see the women moving about, cooking or sitting with their sewing. A man knelt behind his wife on a tarp and started kneading her shoulder with the point of his elbow. She rolled her head back and moaned. Children ran every direction with the usual pack of loose hunting dogs. The dogs stopped when they smelled him and set to barking with their hackles up but nobody paid them any mind.

To his surprise there was no sentry standing watch at the gate. Such a thing would never happen at a Russian fort. Lukin kept moving with his head down, trying to look like a man with somewhere to be, but yet not in too much of a hurry. As he approached, two Canadians exited and started down the path to the riverfront. They wore canvas trousers that had at one time been white and moccasins of a style he'd never seen before with what appeared to be long flaps that wrapped up around their calves and made fast with leather whangs. One wore a red English-style shirt with a black waistcoat, the other a blue and white striped shirt with a paisley kerchief tied round his neck. On his head he wore what Lukin in his colonial Russian knew as a sombrero. It was a word his father's generation had borrowed from the Spanish Californios; in Russian America it just meant any sort of broad-brimmed felt hat. Both men wore colorful sashes wrapped in several turns around their waists.

"Bonjour," said the one in the striped shirt as they passed; he must have seen Lukin studying him.

Lukin nodded and entered the palisade, wondering if those men had been at Nuklukayet. He wanted to stop and look around but there was the imperative to be inconspicuous. Quite suddenly he felt more alone than he had ever been before. At first glance he could see maybe a dozen white men, or at least men who dressed in white men's clothes. More than a couple seemed to be mixed-bloods like himself, and he spied at least two who appeared to be Indians of a different ethnic stock than the Dinneh, though for all he knew they might have been from Cuba. To his utter astonishment, there was even a black-skinned man he recognized as an American Negro. He had heard of them but had never seen one and it took considerable effort to keep his eyes elsewhere.

There were also a number of Quarreler men milling about the courtyard. Some appeared to be working as day laborers helping the British with packing and baling the previous season's fur take for transport. It was a labor-intensive operation that Lukin recognized instantly. They had a fur press made from upright logs buried into the earth. He watched as two Canadians stacked a series of beaver pelts between the flat boards, then wrapped the stack in canvas. Four Quarreler men grabbed hold of the long spring lever and slowly muscled it down to squeeze all the air from the pelts. They held the lever in place while one of the foreign Indians wrapped a series of rawhide straps around the bale and tied them off tight.

The buildings were constructed of logs hewn square and whitewashed. The windows were neatly painted with red trim. He moved off to the side of the gate and hunkered down to make himself as invisible as possible while he studied the architecture and the fort's layout. To his right were a series of three low-slung apartments that he guessed to be the workmen's quarters. To his left were three more rooms, one of which was likely the store and merchandise counter, judging from the people who came and went, generally exiting with some tobacco or a knife or blanket.

Straight back from the courtyard at the rear of the enclosure he spied a large building. *Likely the bidarshik's quarters,* he thought. Possibly it also housed some sort of mess hall; Russian laborers did their own cooking in the fort bunkhouse, but these men's quarters were too small for anything resembling a pitchka which by the nature of its construction dominated a room. Surely they had to sleep at least five to a room.

Flanking the sides of the bidarshik's house was a drying rack covered over with a roof of peeled birchbark flattened down with poles, along with a very large building whose purpose, he surmised, was a fur warehouse, or maybe boat storage. Or possibly both. Rather than planks on the ground to bridge the mud as he was accustomed to in the Russian world, wood chips from the ceaseless woodchopping were strewn about the yard in a thick layer.

This was no mere camp slashed into the forest, but a substantial undertaking backed by significant capital. Lukin's initial impression was that the fort was much better managed and infinitely cleaner than any fur post he had ever been to, especially with the whitewashed finish. What a contrast it was from the dingy yellow walls and red metal roofs of Russian America Company facilities, or the unpainted squalor of places like Nulato. And the wood chips in particular seemed like an obvious idea. He'd never once thought of collecting them for such a purpose and like all obvious ideas it left him feeling both inspired and a little sheepish.

But he could feel something growing inside him. A certainty that whatever else his life may have been in the past, here in front of him was the future. And not just any future, but a future with meaning where he was in control of his own destiny. Why work as a bidarshik for the Russian America Company when the best he could hope for was a modest pension when he was finally too old and used up to be of further service? It seemed the gold offered by Furuhjelm had been more about inducing him to come back downriver than payment for a job well done.

Out in the courtyard at the fur press, one of the Canadians said something and the crew of Quarrelers smirked with laughter. Lukin rubbed a hand over his mouth, working the various angles of what had to happen. He'd walked in the gate still more or less on assignment for the Company and now it seemed he was swimming toward a waterfall. There was Ilya to consider and how to get him upriver. Iriana, he decided in the moment, might as well stay downriver; there was no love left in their marriage anyway. But for now the first thing to do was to find the British bidarshik.

Nobody seemed to be paying him any attention, so he rose and walked behind the men's housing where there was a narrow avenue between the walls and the palisade. At the end of the lane stood an outhouse. Lukin slipped around the side and glanced into the warehouse as he passed. There would be time enough for that later. He was enough on edge that the chill in his damp clothes didn't bother him.

He was walking straight for the door of the bidarshik's office when someone called out in French. Lukin ignored it and raised his arm to knock when a hand grabbed his wrist. He turned to see a pair of Canadians squinting at him.

The one holding his arm said something.

Lukin shook his head. "I don't understand," he said in Russian. "I am here to see the bidarshik."

The Canadians looked at one another then peered at his face. The one not holding onto Lukin turned and rapped on the door.

Everyone in the yard was by now watching. One of the Canadians waved over a Quarreler and spoke to him in a garbled mix of tongues, none of which were comprehensible to Lukin. The man asked him something, of which Lukin understood not a word. He was for a very brief moment irrationally angry at the giant for limiting him to the languages of the downriver country, none of which seemed to have any utility whatsoever up here. It flashed across his mind that he would need to learn not just English, but French as well.

Lukin spoke to the Quarreler man in Denakeh. "Do you have anyone here who speaks the downriver language?"

The Quarreler frowned and said something and pointed outside the palisade. The Canadians nodded, and the Quarreler trotted across the yard and out the gate with his thick queue bobbing and the soft slapping of the fringe on his shirt. The Canadians opened the door and marched Lukin inside. One of them turned and called out to the crowd; Lukin didn't need to speak the language to understand that he'd told them to get back to work.

They entered what did indeed look like a large mess hall, with a pair of long tables running the length and a large hearth for cooking. The door to the bidarshik's office was off to one side. Lukin noted that the inside walls were whitewashed as well, which undoubtedly helped the candlelight go further in winter. The taller of the Canadians knocked on the office door and was told to enter. The other man kept holding onto Lukin's arm and the back of his shirt as they waited. He was not exactly menacing, but it was clear enough that Lukin would do best to not stir things up.

"I'm not here to cause trouble," Lukin told him. "I have a proposition for your boss." He may as well have been talking to a tree stump.

The door opened again and they were waved into the office. Their bidarshik was a trim man a few years younger than Lukin. He appeared to be in the middle of tidying up his office; wooden crates full of paperwork and ledgers were piled up in one corner. A broom made from locally cut grass lashed to an aspen pole leaned against his desk. He sat on the edge of the wood, riffling through a jumbled sheaf of pages that he tipped toward the light of the open window for easier reading.

The man was obviously of a different racial stock than the swarthy Canadians who stood back at arm's length; he was clean-shaven and his yellow hair had been barbered within the last month. When he spoke it was a different language than the Canadians used, and Lukin took this to be English. He'd never heard it before.

The man who'd gone first into the office said something to his boss; the bidarshik switched to French for his reply. Lukin looked around the room. Two very large glass windows faced the courtyard. A stone furnace stood at the back wall, built along the same lines as a Russian pitchka but with a taller, narrower shape. Next to it there was another door that he surmised led to the boss's sleeping chamber. Behind the desk was a tall cabinet with a lock on the door and two shelves lined with ledgers and folders. The British bidarshik studied Lukin for a long moment then walked around the desk to his chair and took his seat. He laced his fingers together atop a folder of papers. All the while he spoke back and forth with the Canadians in French.

There were footsteps. The Quarreler who had gone out had returned, bringing with him a man who Lukin recognized straight off as a Dinneh mixed-blood.

The British bidarshik pointed at Lukin and voiced a question.

Lukin was relieved when the mixed-blood man started speaking in Denakeh. "They've asked me to translate."

"Ah," Lukin said. "Good." He hoped his trepidation didn't show. The windows had been propped open and were large enough to jump through, but he wasn't sure he could get away if they tried to seize him.

"This trader's name is Strachan Jones. He wants to know who you are and why you're here."

Lukin had the sudden thought that perhaps he should have taken the time to concoct an alias for himself. His mind went utterly blank with everyone looking at him and he said, entirely out of long habit, "My name is Ivan Semyonovich Lukin." It seemed like as good a moment as any to lay his cards on the table.

"You're a Russian?" the translator said.

"Yes. I wish to speak to your bidarshik about defecting."

"Bidarshik?"

"This man." Lukin gestured at Jones. "The boss."

The translator raised an eyebrow at him, then related this to Jones. Jones spoke back in English, and the translator answered him in kind. Lukin heard the word *Russian* and his name.

Jones moved his eyes over to Lukin. He spoke.

"He says, Why would you do such a thing?"

"I work for the Russian America Company. My employer sent me up here to spy on your operations. But now I'm thinking I might prefer to work for you."

A series of emotions washed over Jones' face, none of them especially pleasant to watch. There was anger, then calculation, then narrow-eyed suspicion.

"Why would I hire a man who was sent to spy on me?" the translator said with a practiced tone.

"Because I know the river," Lukin said. Technically he'd only been up the Kwifpak once, but they didn't need to know that. "I was born and raised here in Russian America, and I know the Russian trade backward and forward." He inclined his head, looking Jones in the eye. "I can be of good use to you, Bidarshik."

Jones looked over at the translator, then back at Lukin. He smoothed the stubble on his lip with a thumb and forefinger, then covered his mouth with his palm, thinking. When he spoke it was slow and deliberate.

"He wants to know why you want to help him," said the translator.

Lukin planted his hands on his hips. "I have been ill-used by my employer of late. I'm looking for a new start." He gestured out the window, around the fort facilities. "I grew up in the fur trade, and I speak all the downriver languages. I have contacts with the Denakeh and the Koltsan over the mountains to the south. And I like the look of your operation here."

Upon hearing the translation Jones rose and walked to the window. The sky was beginning to break up; out in the yard a line of cloud shadow crept across the ground. He clasped his hands behind his back, keeping his eyes outside as he spoke.

"He says, How many years have you worked for the Russian traders?"

"Most of my life. My father was the bidarshik at Fort Kolmakov. The Company started paying me a salary when I was fourteen."

Jones spoke again.

"He wants to know if you can make words on paper." The translator pointed at the stacks of papers. There was no elegant way to say it in Denakeh.

Jones turned from the window. Lukin pantomimed holding a pin and scribbling it against his open palm. "Yes," he said, nodding emphatically at Jones.

The translator spoke again after listening to Jones. "How many languages do you speak?"

Lukin held up the five fingers of his right hand. "Russian and Denakeh, of course. Also Koltsan, Deghitan, and Yupiak. That's the language of the people on the lower Kuskokwim and Kwifpak rivers."

"But not English," Jones said through the translator. "Or French or Kutchin."

"No." Lukin lifted the corner of his mouth. "But I learn fast." He chose to ignore the fact that these tongues were outside the limits of his linguistic power. He listened as Jones spoke, wishing to hell he could talk directly to the man. English sounded like geese cackling at one another.

"He wants to know what manner of work you do for the Russian Company."

Lukin had lost all sense of how this conversation was drifting. It was tempting to tell Jones that he'd once been a bidarshik like him and that he knew firsthand how taxing the job was. Then again, you didn't really want to talk about your failures during a job interview. And when he got right down to it, he wasn't precisely sure what his job title was these days.

"I am what we call prikazchik. That's a sort of assistant who works as a field agent. I travel among the Natives and encourage them to bring their furs in to sell."

The bidarshik pursed his lips as he listened to the translation, then walked back to his desk, speaking as he went.

"He presumes you're looking for work similar to what you did for the Russians."

Lukin nodded. "Your fort stands on Russian soil. You know this as well as I do. The Russian America Company and the Czar intend to come up here with soldiers and drive you back into Rupert's Land. It would be to your advantage to have a Russian on your staff."

The tone of Lukin's voice brought a frown of incomprehension to Jones' face. Even the translator didn't seem to know what to make of it. One of the Canadians spoke in French and Jones answered in kind, then he switched back to English and spoke at length.

The translator sighed a little. "He says he does not doubt that you are a capable trader, but he cannot give you a job. He says he would never know if you were working for him or for the Russians."

Lukin looked down at the floor. He had to work hard to keep from clenching his fists. "Anything else?"

"Yes. He says he could take you a prisoner and ransom you to your countrymen. Or have you taken to Montreal and executed."

Lukin's pulse quickened in his ears. Nobody was holding onto him, and if he was going to make a move out the open window now was the moment.

"But," said the translator, "he desires peace and the tolerance of our Russian neighbors, so he will let you go."

A hot feeling of foolishness crept up from Lukin's feet as it slowly dawned on him that here was one more thing he had failed at.

Jones said something that was translated as, "The Hudson Bay Company wishes you a good day and a safe journey home."

Lukin turned sharply and shoved aside the Canadian who tried to slow him down, but the two of them got hold of his arms and frogmarched him outside. Everyone in the yard stopped what they were doing once again to watch as the unmasked Russian was escorted across the yard. Lukin pulled against them, wanting nothing so much as to bolt for the water and find Zia to finally give his soul over to her. There was a vague notion that he was trying to outrun the shame that was bound to follow him downriver. He might have called out Zia's name in the moment as he struggled and several pairs of hands gripped his limbs and balled up into the leather of his shirt and dragged him across the wood chips. Also the title Queen of Cups, though he was even less certain about that one.

New raindrops splattered onto his skin as they finally turned him loose outside the gate. Down by the waterfront the lavender blossoms atop the fireweed swayed in the breeze.

6

DOWNRIVER AGAIN — SHADOW OF HIS FATHER — ANOTHER FAILURE — A HOLE IN THE SKY — CROW AND THE RUFFED GROUSE GIRL — MANUMISSION — BLANKET HOUSE — THE NEW BRIDE — NO JOB IS FINISHED UNTIL THE PAPERWORK IS DONE — VISIT FROM THE GROOM — COLONIAL WEDDING — THE WORM TURNS — FESTIVITIES — ILYA TO BED — RUM AND WATER — THE QUEEN OF CUPS — POETICS — KURILA'S VIVID IMAGINATION — GORKO

The Dinneh tribes had a story of Crow building a giant raft to hold all the animals of the forest during a flood that covered the entire Earth, but neither that story nor the version with Noah offered much in the way of guidance when your efforts in life came to naught and you were stuck in a canoe with the dreariness of the August rain and the pulsing edge of your own inadequacy.

Failure, it seemed, was the dominant theme of his life. What would Semyon Lukin have done, Semyon Lukin who had enjoyed success at every turn in his life? Lukin didn't much care, but everyone else in Russian America certainly would. And the only ones who wouldn't have cared were back upriver at Fort Youcon.

It took him three days to descend to the top of the ramparts. Near his camp he spied a very fresh bull moose track in the sand and spent nearly a whole day and most of the night trailing it through the dripping woods with his gunlock clamped into his armpit to keep the charge dry. He tried a few grunts and some scraping of the willows to mimic the antics of a rival bull, but it was still too early in the season for it to have the desired effect. Failure again.

He stood up from his hiding place at the edge of a broad open muskeg and for no particular reason reached into his jacket pocket and fingered the blue bead that had been there, forgotten, since May. The scraggly black spruce leaned at various angles around him as he pulled it out and cupped it in his palm. "Be the blue sky," he said. It was a forlorn prayer but to his surprise a hole opened in the clouds.

The rain slowly tapered off and the sky broke up as he slogged his way back to the river, stopping periodically to admire the last of the wildflowers as morning sunshine again filled the forest. His mind felt like the skin had been peeled back to reveal the most tender tissue to the hard air of the world. Flowers at least were one of the true joys of summertime and he was particularly fond of the tiny pearls of water that collected on the inner petals where the bumblebees came to land. They crawled about in the powdery centers, wallowing like little furry pigs.

He stopped just inside the edge of the birch forest when he saw her sitting on the beach. She had her legs drawn up with her arms wrapped around them and as usual was looking out at the river. The ends of her matted hair had piled up behind her with wet sand clinging to the locks.

Lukin pushed through the grass and fireweed at the edge of the gravel and walked down the beach. "Good day, Zia."

She smiled up at him. "You look wet and miserable."

He managed a small chuckle. "That's very perceptive of you."

"Sit with me." She patted the sand at her left side. Lukin complied, slipping his powderhorn and shotpouch over his head and propping his gun against them to keep the lock out of the grit.

He looked out at the river from where she'd come. Zia reached out and pushed a string of his wet hair back from his head. A chill ran through him, probably from his wet clothes, and there was no way to avoid thoughts of the winter that was coming.

"What troubles you?" she asked.

Lukin sighed a little, still listening the whisperings of the river's current. He'd been fascinated by water and the sounds it made from his very earliest memories and he wondered if this was how Zia was always able to find him. Perhaps how she had found him from the very beginning.

Her eyes were large and dark as she blinked at him. It made her seem close enough to human. "Were you watching me at Fort Youcon?"

"I was."

"So you know what happened."

She nodded.

"Would I have been happy living among the British?"

"Who knows?"

"The Company will send me back to St. Michael now that this assignment is done."

"Is that so bad?"

"I loathe St. Michael." The treeless tundra of the coast always made him unhappy, and in his mind he could hear Iriana carping at him and blaming him for every little thing that went wrong. Plunking his dinner plate down in front of him and sitting in silence with her sewing while he ate, pointedly not looking at him, then fixing herself a plate when he went up to the loft to bed. Her coming up late with a candle and blowing it out and getting under the covers. Flinching if he touched her. All the arguments conducted in whispers so as to not wake Ilya.

"I'll be there with you," Zia said, inching closer to him. The air around them was damp and close, but the space between them seemed filled with warmth.

Lukin had nothing to say in any language as she leaned into him and planted her lips upon his. Her kiss was pliant, with all the impatience of youth. He'd never allowed himself to dwell on thoughts of such a thing with Zia—she was barely more than a girl and he had a daughter her age—but with her tongue sliding against his and her scent filling his head this suddenly seemed a trivial concern. Her hand slid up to the back of his neck and she buried her fingers into his hair beneath its queue. He was aware of a sliding sensation, like being pulled by the current of a river toward the sea, and there was a Deghitan town on the Kuskokwim River and Semyon standing with an older man Lukin recognized as his other grandfather, the chieftain he knew only as Tixyaa. The houses were built into the ground with short walls of cut spruce logs and roofs of birchbark and out from a door came a young woman in a new dress of caribou fawnskins trimmed in fringe and strips of mink fur. It was late summer, probably August from the look of the sunlight and the topmost blooms of the fireweed and when she stood up straight from exiting the house he recognized her instantly as his mother. She didn't look at her father, or at Semyon as she followed him to the canoe waiting to take them back downriver to make the arduous journey up the Hohlitna River and back to Fort Aleksandr.

The fireweed tops were in bloom and the gathered crowd followed them down to the gravel beach like a gang of seagulls with new steel knives and axes and copper cooking pots. Tears pooled in the corners of Lukin's eyes to see his mother again, not careworn and homesick for her country but young and pretty and full of life.

They got into Semyon's canoe loaded with furs. Six more canoes loaded with peltry floated in the shallows; the Creole boatmen watched their boss and his new wife. Semyon indicated she should take the bow and she did so and as they started paddling Lukin could see her thinking of her sewing kit stashed away in her gear. Of the story from the Distant Time when Crow disguised himself as a wealthy man by scraping together a bunch of fish bones and dog turds and using magic to make it into a suit of fine clothes. How he used this magic to marry a chief's daughter and as they paddled away in Crow's canoe and got around the first bend his power started wearing off and the bride could see his clothes turning back into bones and shit so she silently pulled out her awl and sewed the tail of his shirt to the canoe thwart. And when they pulled into shore at his miserable camp she bolted for the forest and he went to leap after her but was held fast by her tight stitches, shouting and cursing at her as she ran home.

Maybe if I can ride in the stern, his mother thought as she paddled and watched the lavender smear of fireweed blooms on the distant bank. Then again, in the story Crow got loose and found her hidden on a cache platform and drove his lance up into her heart between the poles. As her blood ran down the shaft she changed into a ruffed grouse and flew away into the woods. *If I die,* Lukin's mother mused, *could I change into a bird so I can stay in my country?*

Lukin had seen such visions from Zia for many years but had never before heard anyone's thoughts. Zia slid her arms around his neck and straddled his lap, gripping him tighter. The world filled with a thrumming sensation that you felt in your gut and the moon had drawn closer, filling the entire sky with its mouth open and its teeth gleaming. She started pushing Lukin down to the sand when Crow turned to look at him. His hair was glossy and his eyes showed no whites or iris, only the blackness of the sky on a moonless night and you could see the stars inside them. Then he blinked and the shirt of trash fell away as he flapped his wings up to the sun.

Zia's kisses had become insistent to the point of chewing. A dissonant sound ripped through the air as Lukin shoved her away and rolled back. He stood up, panting. A wave of nausea spread through him and it was all he could do to stay on his feet. The moon's face pulled down in anger as it hovered over the treetops filling the sky like a ceiling. Zia sat up on her knees, lips parted, and crooked a finger at him, beckoning him into her.

"Go away," Lukin said. "This is not what I want."

"Yes it is."

"Get away from me!" he shouted at her. It sounded almost plaintive.

"This is a mistake you do not want to make, Ivan."

Lukin looked up at the moon and drew the dagger from the sheath around his neck. Slowly it pulled back into the depth of the sky. When he looked back for Zia she was gone. Only a series of ripples in the river showed where she'd left as he sank down to his knees and lowered his head against the damp river beach until the nausea passed.

* * *

In the early days at Fort Kolmakov, Semyon and his son Ivan Lukin would head up the Kuskokwim each April to trade with the Koltsan, taking one or two laborers from the fort and driving teams of their worst dogs. They spent breakup building canoes, then killed the dogs and traded all through May and June at a cabin they'd built the forks before floating back down to the fort. This was in the days when Semyon was still in his youthful prime and the Company imported scores of new sled dogs every year from Kamchatka.

It was on one of these trips that Lukin met Iriana. This was 1845, not long after his voyage across the Bering Sea with the Chinese bureaucrat's head. Grigori Tretiakov, the fort carpenter, came with them that year, for in addition to the usual fur buying, he and Semyon Lukin had plans to arrange a marriage between Ivan Lukin and Tretiakov's eldest daughter Natalia. She had never been very fond of Fort Kolmakov and spent as much time as she could living with her Koltsan relatives upriver. One of those relatives—her grandfather—just happened to be the principal chief of the Koltsan.

On the third night after the arrival of their customers, while the Russians sat around their fire outside the cabin, smoking and talking of Ivan Lukin's betrothal, an aging Koltsan matron came up leading a slave girl by a moosehide leash around her neck. This took everyone by surprise but Semyon.

"Auntie," he said. "I see you've brought me something."

"I need more tobacco and beads," the woman said. Lukin remembered her from a couple years back. A grizzly had surprised them picking berries and he'd watched, stunned, as her nephew killed it with his spear after taunting and throwing sticks at it to make it charge.

"I beg your pardon?" said Semyon.

"More tobacco and beads. Those large blue ones."

"Auntie, we already agreed on the price. Six kettles, six axes, six blankets, twenty strings of blue beads, and a gun for your nephew next summer."

This was no trifling sum, but the matron frowned and shook her head. "She tans excellent leather. I taught her myself. And she's a first-rate seamstress. She's worth more."

"She's Yupiak," Grigori whispered to Lukin.

The word technically meant the language the coastal people spoke, not the people themselves. But he was right—she wore a filthy castoff Dinneh woman's dress, but her face was too round for a Dinneh, with pronounced epicanthic folds at the corners of her eyes. It went unsaid that Semyon Lukin's boyhood experience as a slave among the Kolosh had marked him. He'd inoculated his children with the belief that keeping slaves was both sinful and morally indefensible. The example he continually cited was the United States of America. A degenerate upstart of a nation, he called it, full to the brim with its own hypocrisy and bullshit.

There was just enough slack in the line for the girl to keep her chin down against her chest. She glanced briefly at Ivan Lukin and he looked away.

Semyon Lukin folded his arms over his chest. "You said yourself that she needs a beating every couple days to keep her working. If I pay a fair price for a slave, I shouldn't get one that makes me break a sweat whipping her all the time. If I'm going to be that tired at the end of the day, I could just do the work myself."

"She works hard," the matron said. "She just requires the proper motivation. And besides, it feels good to whip a misbehaving slave."

"Alright, Auntie," Semyon Lukin sighed. "You drive a hard bargain." He rose and went into the house, emerging with the additional tobacco and a string of blue beads. The woman laid the leash into his hand, then smirked at the girl as she took her leave.

"Do you speak Koltsan?" Semyon asked as he drew his knife and cut the bonds at her wrists.

She nodded.

He loosened the leash and slipped it over her head. "And Yupiak?"

She looked up at him, astonished. "Yes."

"What is your name?"

"Kaymaq."

"I'm Semyon Lukin. This is Grigori Tretiakov, Natalia's father. And that's my son, Ivan Lukin. Please, sit."

She watched him like a scared animal.

"Nobody is going to beat you anymore," Semyon said. "I purchased you to set you free."

"Am I to be a wife?" she asked in Yupiak as she sank to the ground.

"Only if you want to be. I'm sure we can help you find a good husband."

"Him?" she gestured at Ivan Lukin.

Semyon smiled. "I'm afraid my son is betrothed to Natalia Tretiakova. But I know plenty of other good men."

"Oh."

"I thought you might like to come back to Fort Kolmakov with us. We can help you sort something out down there. Maybe help you get home to your people."

She said nothing more, and it was Lukin's initial impression that she had forgotten how to smile. There was talk between Semyon and Grigori, and eventually they got up and went inside to call it a night. She and Ivan Lukin watched them go.

"You're not going to bed?" she said. Lukin spoke good Yupiak and he could hear that she was having difficulty with it. This he reckoned must be a source of distress for her.

"I'm not sleepy."

"Why not?"

"Sometimes I don't sleep."

"I guess you're maybe worried about something."

He snorted a rather unhappy laugh. This was the early years of Zia's presence in his life, and he'd been awake talking to her for a series of nights. She had showed him a vision over and over of his father administering a flogging to an Aleut worker with Baranov looking on in stern approval. On two separate occasions he'd caught her creeping toward the camp where his father slept and had been so dazed by what he'd seen that it had been hard to steer her away from the others. For all he knew, she was watching them right now.

"Yes, I am," he said.

Kaymaq was silent for a moment, keeping her eyes on the earth in front of her. "So you and Natalia are to be married."

He poked a stick into the fire to get more air into the coals. The flames leapt up. "Yes. My father and Grigori and her aunts have arranged it."

"You don't look very happy about it."

"It is what the Company requires. Her grandfather is an important trading partner for us."

"What is the Company?"

"The group of fur buyers for whom we work. They're all back in Russia and New Archangel."

"She's really pretty. All the boys want her."

"I suppose she is. But looks aren't everything." He stabbed the poker stick into the dirt next to his feet. "I suppose I had hoped to choose my own bride. For love."

A tear rolled down Kaymaq's cheek, then another. Lukin had no answer for this but he reached out and brushed her filthy hair away from her eyes. "Take heart."

Later that summer, Kaymaq was baptized into the Orthodox Church at Fort Kolmakov by Father Netsvetov. She was given the name of Iriana. Ivan Lukin and Natalia Tretiakova were wed the next day.

* * *

The fireweed had shed its summer flowers and the leaves were just beginning to turn scarlet. Its cottony seeds drifted over the water in the barest of breezes and mist rose from the back sloughs in the chilly mornings. Everyone came down to the beach at Nulato to meet Lukin's solitary canoe and he was heartened to see Ilya dragging Iriana by her hand down to the water's edge. His son was the one bright spot left in his world and he nearly cried when he picked the lad up and held him close. His hair was longer and somewhere in the summer he had started to look much more like a little kid than a baby boy. Given the way time moved, Lukin expected that within the week his son would be trimming his beard and announcing that he was moving out of the house to get married.

"We can go in the blanket house, Papa?"

Lukin blinked a few times at his son. He'd feared the lad would have outgrown such a thing. "Of course we can," he said, ruffling the boy's hair. He thought he might actually weep.

Iriana's hug was perfunctory, performed mostly for the sake of appearances. She said, "I missed you," looking out at the river as she spoke, perhaps wishing he'd passed Nulato and just kept on going. All the same the scent of her tugged at him, for better or for worse.

"I missed you too, my love."

Sava and Denisov made their way to the front of the crowd to offer handshakes and kisses. Denisov even handed Lukin a loaf of black bread and a leather bag of salt to make him welcome, an old custom from Russia that had taken root in the colony. Lukin couldn't help but wonder if word of his perfidy had somehow filtered downriver ahead of him and it added a somewhat sour note to the backslaps and handshakes that came from all directions.

Even Metrikov softened a little. He came through the crowd with a bottle of rum and poured a toast for the entire fort crew. "To Ivan Semyonovich Lukin," he said, raising his cup into the air.

"Lukin!" came the cry.

Lukin was still holding Ilya against him as he threw back the rum. His eye caught a familiar face. "Is that the lady from Nowikaket?" he asked Sava. "Deryabin's daughter?"

She wore a new-made Russian sarafan dress with a white chemise, wrapped tight around her waist with what appeared to be a sash from the Hudson Bay Company like he'd seen the Canadian boatmen wearing. Below the calf-length hem were a pair of fitted leggings with the moccasins sewn on in the common fashion. The clothes themselves were nothing unusual but they were a marked contrast from the shabby mourning attire he'd last seen her in.

"Anfisa, yes." Sava replied.

"She's come back to Nulato?"

"Indeed. She and Yosif are getting married."

"You don't say." It was always disarming to be away for an extended period, only to find on your return that things had shifted so far in your absence.

"Yosif!" he called out to Denisov who had moved up next to his fiancée and slipped his arm around her waist. "What is this about you getting married?"

"You're just in time," he said back. "It's happening on Saturday. If Father Netsvetov gets here. We were hoping he would already be here."

"What day is today?" Lukin asked.

"It's Tuesday," Iriana said.

"Hell's bells. I thought it was maybe Friday."

Anfisa met his eyes for the briefest of moments, then looked away as Metrikov began pouring out a second round. Lukin reached over and planted a kiss on Iriana's cheek and she at least had the courtesy to smile and pretend she appreciated it. He tried not to think of the argument he knew was coming. There was always an argument when he got home from a trip.

* * *

Paperwork was as much a never-ending part of life in the fur trade as being gone from your family, especially when you worked within the byzantine bureaucracy of the Russian America Company. Lukin spent the next several days sitting at the table in his quarters drafting a report of his trip to Fort Youcon. This was made considerably more difficult because Iriana was now spending most of her time in Sergei Metrikov's house; he quickly grasped that his wife had been sleeping in the bidarshik's bed, and Sava unhappily confirmed this when he asked. This left Lukin with the responsibility of looking after Ilya, as well as enduring the whispers of the fort's residents about his personal business.

At least his insomnia meant he could stay up most of the night working when Ilya was asleep. Iriana came around to bring them their supper, then she departed, leaving Lukin to wonder if she was only interested in bedding with the bull of the woods, something he clearly no longer was. At least it only hurt when she walked away; beyond that there was only a species of dull numbness and a powerful urge to whitewash the interior walls of his cabin. Sadly, there was no lime to be had for such a project.

On Thursday morning he'd just started on the second copy of the report when Ilya came up and propped his elbows over his father's thigh like he was standing at a bar.

"What are you doing, Papa?"

"I'm working."

"Blanket house?"

Lukin smiled and sighed a little. Who was he to deny his son's happiness? "Alright. Go get the blanket."

It was an old Hudson Bay blanket, white with multicolor stripes at either end, given to him and Iriana as a wedding gift. He and Ilya settled themselves on the floor against the nearby wall and Ilya climbed up into his lap. Lukin threw one end over the back of the chair and tucked the other between his back and the dingy log wall. The white blanket let plenty of light in to see as he touched Ilya's cheek.

"Tell me a story, Papa," the boy said.

"A story?"

"Yes."

Lukin pursed his lips in thought. "Have you heard about Crow and the Goose Girl?" Raven stories had been in his mind lately.

"No."

"So, long ago in the Distant Time Crow fell in love with a goose girl. Her people were up here for the summer and they were busy being young and in love when her father announced it was time for all the geese to leave and fly south."

Ilya's dark eyes watched him with their usual intensity.

"Naturally Crow wanted to fly south with his lady, but her father wouldn't have it. He said, 'The journey is long and we have to carry our young ones. I don't think you will make it.' So Crow took off into the air to demonstrate how well he could fly." Lukin flattened his palm and banked it to and fro inside the blanket house to demonstrate. "He flew this way and that, way high up in the sky so far they could barely see him, then he turned a bunch of somersaults and came back down and spread his wings to catch the air and fly again. Then he landed and said, 'I can help you all on the trip. When I wish for something, it always comes true.'"

"Because he's Crow," Ilya said.

"Exactly. So Goose Girl's father finally agreed to let him come with them. They took off and at first Crow did fine. But he's not built for long-distance flying. Before they were even halfway over the ocean he started getting tired all the time. Goose Girl's father and brothers took turns carrying him, but then they started getting tired and there was nowhere to land for a rest."

Ilya had been patting his hands against his thighs, getting restless. "What happened?"

"They had to let him go so they could finish the journey. It was either that or fall to the ocean with him."

"It must have made Goose Girl really sad."

"I'm sure it did. And it must have been terrible for Crow to be plummeting down toward the sea and looking into her eyes the whole time."

"What happened then?"

"That's a story for some other time. But right now I have to get back to work." Watching Ilya stand up and duck out of the blanket house, Lukin reckoned Goose Girl's father was probably happy to be rid of her big-talking paramour. But that was a perspective that came with age and fatherhood.

That afternoon when he'd just put Ilya down for his nap there came a rap at the door. Lukin looked up to see Yosif Denisov holding a bottle of rum.

"Ivan," Denisov said.

Lukin put a finger to his lips and pointed upward at the loft.

Denisov lowered his voice. "Little Ilya?"

Lukin nodded. Denisov carefully unlatched the lower half of the Dutch door and let himself in. He held up the bottle. "This was a wedding present from Metrikov. I thought you should have a taste."

"You look like you've had a taste already." By long tradition in the colony, both bride and groom were encouraged to start the celebration early. Denisov wasn't fully drunk but he had at least a couple in him. Lukin set his pen down and corked his inkwell and got up and to retrieve a couple of mugs.

Denisov's snort stopped him. "What are we, French?"

Lukin turned back as Denisov pushed the bottle out at him. He set the cups back on the shelf. "As you like, Captain." He lifted the bottle by the neck. "To the bride and groom." Denisov beamed as Lukin tipped a healthy swig into his mouth and passed it back.

Denisov took a drink, then wiped his lips with his jacketsleeve. He set the bottle down onto the tabletop. "Doing your paperwork, I see."

"Yes. The damn Company should go into the stationary business and gain a monopoly on the whole world."

"I came to hear about your trip."

"Keep your voice down, if you please."

"Yes, sorry. Tell me what you saw at Fort Youcon."

"The buildings there are all whitewashed with red trim. They spread wood chips around the courtyard to keep their feet out of the mud."

"By God, I never thought of that."

Lukin smiled politely down at the table.

"It seems like such an obvious thing to do," Denisov said.

"I know."

"Drink up."

"I'm fine."

Denisov pushed the rum across the table to Lukin. "Drink if you want me to be quiet."

Lukin thought in the moment that his old friend was in fact not a very pleasant drunk, but he took a drink and set the bottle back down.

"Did you take Sava's advice?" Denisov asked, reaching for the rum.

"Sava's advice?"

"To tell the Hudson Bay bidarshik you were a deserter from the Russian America Company."

Lukin was still looking at the table as his smile slid away. "I did."

* * *

The Nulato community grew more and more festive in anticipation of Denisov and Anfisa's wedding. Father Netsvetov arrived late on Friday from the Orthodox mission at Ikogmiut and the whole fort breathed a sigh of relief that the party would not have to be delayed. It was hot and stuffy inside the crude log chapel—none of the windows opened and the tiny space was crammed tight with bodies so that the front row was very near standing on the red cloth in the center of the chapel where the bride and groom stood with the priest and their witnesses. Those who couldn't fit peered in through the open door, rising up on their tiptoes to see the only daughter of Vasili Deryabin in her wedding finery.

In Russia or Siberia the betrothal ceremony would have been a separate affair held when the couple were first engaged, but in the American colony when the priest might only come around once in a year it was done right before the main event of the crowning ceremony. Netsvetov performed the blessing, then handed lighted candles to the bride and groom. For rings they could only muster a pair of the cheap copper ones sold to the Natives. These the priest placed on their right hands.

Anfisa had selected Sonia Rudinova to be her witness and Denisov had tapped Sava. Each held their wedding crown over the head of their charge while the litany was recited, along with several prayers. Netsvetov had been the parish priest of the Kwifpak district for nearly twenty years, and the crowns traveled with him. Lukin and Iriana had both worn those same crowns eight years before when they wed.

Lukin was holding Ilya so he could see, despite the fact that he was getting too big and heavy for it. Iriana was wedged up against him but only because of the packed sweaty space and the fact that it would not do for her to be seen with Metrikov while the priest was around. All but the priest and the bride and groom stood with their heads uncovered before God. Watching Anfisa, Lukin couldn't stop himself from wondering if her leggings went all the way up to where we all come from, or if they stopped just above the knee leaving her thighs and the rest of her bare underneath the dress. He was aghast to feel his worm stiffen at the imagery. In church with his wife standing against him, no less.

The wedding feast was coho salmon, bear meat for those who were not tabooed from eating it, potatoes from the garden, golden-fried in grease, and the last greens from the summer's kitchen patch. This time of year there was still plenty of flour and sugar to bake a cake, and several of Anfisa's extended Dinneh family showed up with pots of grease rendered from caribou bones and whipped up with blueberries and sugar. The lateness of the season notwithstanding, Metrikov had decreed that no work would be done that day so that all could celebrate. As was normal for these things, the party carried on into the fading light of the crisp autumn evening when more wood was piled on the bonfires and the dancers reinvigorated themselves.

Iriana came up to Lukin carrying Ilya. "I'm going to put him down to bed." Her face was softened by the flickering glow of the fire. "Does he feel warm to you?"

Lukin laid a palm on the lad's forehead but he twisted away and buried his face into his mother's neck with a yawn. Lukin had been nursing his grog to keep the pleasant buzzy feeling at a good level without getting soused. It had him feeling warm and expansive, but not quite enough so to ignore the concern in Iriana's eyes.

"He's probably fine," Lukin said. He reached out and stroked the boy's unkempt hair. Ilya yawned again and Lukin moved his hand down to tickle his ribs, but Ilya said, "No," and pushed his hand away.

"I think maybe he's getting sick," Iriana said, feeling their son's cheek with the back of her hand. "And he's tired."

"Hurry back, my star," he called after her as she moved past the fire toward their cabin. He didn't know for sure where she'd be sleeping, but he reckoned she could have the bed if she was staying over and he would just sleep on the floor downstairs. Across the fire Metrikov's eyes watched her depart, then locked onto Lukin's for the briefest of seconds. Lukin was entitled to challenge him to a duel, but then he was weary of the whole thing and decided his boss could have her if he wanted her.

From somewhere in the crowd someone shouted out, "Gorko!" for the bride and groom, and the whole party took up the chant. The word meant *bitter* and the implication was that the bride was looking sour and the groom had better sweeten her up with a kiss. Smiling and rolling his eyes rather dramatically, Denisov stepped over to Anfisa and planted the demanded kiss on her lips as she slid her arms around his neck. Everyone broke out into applause and cheers. Lukin was somewhat unsettled by the flush of lust he'd felt during the ceremony and moved away to sit on a log by the riverbank with his cup of rum and water where he could just see the outlines of the boats traced in the amber firelight. He fingered the blue bead he'd found tucked into the very deepest corner of his jacket pocket, forgotten since early summer. The dark void of the water lay beyond with the soft luffing of the current.

"Captain Lukin."

He twisted around, holding a palm out against the glare of the fire so as to better see. It was a woman with a crown atop her head and a tin cup in her hand. There was the briefest of moments when he saw the Queen of Cups, but then he came back to Earth and stood for the bride. "Madame Denisova."

"You're out here all alone. The party is back there." He could see the faint steam from her breath illuminated by the firelight along the dark edge of her silhouette. Her gait showed her to be just slightly tipsy.

He smiled. "I was watching the stars. We haven't seen them since Easter."

The bonfire behind Anfisa was the brightest light in a thousand-mile radius of country. She lifted her gaze to the heavens. "The September night is always immense after a summer of light."

Lukin tried to think of words to match this poetry but he came up with nothing. *God help me, the snake is on the move again.* It was the curve of her waist set off by the broad sash, the cup of firelight around the line of her chin.

Her wedding ring glinted as she reached up to tuck a strand of her hair behind her ear, underneath the elaborate wedding crown. "So you are the son of the famous Semyon Lukin."

"I am. And I'm told you're the only daughter of Vasili Deryabin."

She blinked at him a few times. When she opened her mouth to speak it took her a moment to form the words. "I never had the chance to thank you for what you did at Nowikaket."

"Think nothing of it. Any gentleman would have done the same." He thought of Lavrov, dead on the beach at Nuklukayet.

"Perhaps. But thank you all the same, Captain."

Lukin nodded and looked over at the fire. "There's no need to be so formal. Your husband is one of my oldest friends."

Anfisa didn't seem to know what to do with her hands. "Anyway, there's something I wanted to ask you about."

"Fire away." He tried to shift his nether regions into a more comfortable position, without success.

"Kurila told me you've been to China."

Lukin tipped his head back. "Oh, good Lord."

"Is it true?"

"It is not true," Lukin said. "When I was a young man the Company sent me on an errand across the sea to the port of Ayan. I stayed the winter, then I came back. I'm not really sure how that got turned into such a wild story." He omitted the nature of his errand, or the sight of the Mongolian herdsman's sword slicing through the Chinese swindler's neck. Nobody at a wedding wanted to hear about a public execution.

"Kurila does have a vivid imagination."

"Anatoli Rudinov has been to China, though. He told me he saw a bear fight a Manchurian tiger inside an iron cage at Maimaicheng."

Anfisa laughed a little. "I've heard that story myself a couple times. He lost a lot of money betting on the fight."

Lukin's eye caught the shape of Iriana, standing in the shadows of the monstrous night and watching him. Even then he knew there was a tectonic shift happening in his life, something that had only just begun at Fort Youcon.

"You should get back to your groom," he said to Anfisa, then raised his voice so all could hear. "Gorko."

Seasons of Want and Plenty: Points of Culture and History

Baranov, that is, Alexander Andreovich Baranov, (the Butcher, as Lukin and his companions often style him) was the first general manager of the Russian America Company. He had previously worked for Grigori Shelhikov, the Company's founder and president, on Kodiak Island where he established a methodology of systematically brutalizing Native people in the quest for sea otter pelts. After his appointment in 1799 he expanded the Company's interests eastward to the Alexander Archipelago (what is today known as Southeast Alaska) by fighting the local Tlingit people to a draw near the present-day city of Sitka (formerly New Archangel).

Latter-day historians have described Baranov as a "complex man," which is what mainstream writers usually say about vile white men who did terrible things in history. Baranov's methods were brutal, even by the standards of the day. He kidnapped wives and children to ensure obedience from husbands and fathers. He raped Native women and encouraged his men to do the same. He split up Native and Creole families by force as suited his whims and purposes, often sending husbands as far away as California and Hawaii against their will. Taking their families with them was never an option; the women and children had to stay under the governor's watchful eye. The fact that he provided contracts that specified payments to their widows and orphans does not change the essential fact that he treated these folks more or less as slaves.

Baranov was removed from power in 1818; after this, the colony was administered by Russian naval officers who served five-year terms on loan from their military service. Aleksandr Baranov died of illness at sea on his way back to face punishment in Russia.

Bidar and bidarka refer to the two most common kinds of boats used by the Russians in their North American colony. A bidar was a large open boat made of walrus skin (*laftak*, in the colonial argot) stretched drum-tight over a wooden frame. It could be moved either by sail or by pairs of oarsmen. This craft was a modified form of the oomiak of the Yup'ik and Inupiaq peoples.

The bidarka was essentially what twenty-first century readers would call a kayak. Like the bidar it was made from laftak stretched over a wooden frame. Bidarkas were originally adopted from the Unangan people of the Aleutian Islands in the 1700s, and proved so handy that the Russians built and used them everywhere they went in Alaska. They were made in configurations with one, two, and three hatches. Boats with laftak shells required regular maintenance to stay watertight, but when used in freshwater for extensive periods the skin would start to break down if not greased every day. Because of this, Russians on the interior rivers often made use of birchbark canoes built in the Athabascan Indian style, with flat bottoms and raked sides.

Bidarshik was the title given to fort managers in Russian America. In the earliest days of the colony, the term referred to the captain of a fleet of bidars (see above). A bidarshik had absolute authority over all of his subordinates, much the same as a ship's captain. There were, at least in theory, limits to what actions he could take and what punishments he could mete out. But God was up in Heaven and the Czar was far away.

Creoles in Russian America were people of mixed Russian and Native parentage. The Russian America Company encouraged its employees to marry and be fruitful with Native women, though how consensual these unions were is perhaps an open question. The Company was tacitly following a proven strategy of the Russian Empire from its conquest of Siberia: impregnate the local women (willingly or not) and produce a class of mixed-blood children who could speak the Native language, understand the culture, and serve as intermediaries, but would remain loyal to the Empire and to Russian cultural norms. The point is often made by historians that there were never more than 800 or so ethnic Russians in Alaska at any given time during the Russian period, but the population of Creoles was much more substantial. They constituted, in effect, the colonial citizenry, and were not infrequently placed in high positions of authority.

The word *Creole* was derived from the Spanish *criollo,* and may have been borrowed from the Spanish settlers of California with whom the Russian America Company had semi-regular interaction. It appears in printed Russian material as early as 1816. Those designated as Creoles paid no taxes. They and their children had the right to an education, paid for by the Company, though it could be argued that the Company provided this education mainly as a way of securing competent employees, something they struggled with throughout their existence.

People of mixed Russian and Native ancestry are still very much resident in Alaska. In recent years, the term Creole has come to be seen by some groups (though not all) as a racist legacy of colonialism in general, and the Russian occupation more specifically. I have elected to use it in these books for the simple reason that Ivan Lukin and his mixed-blood contemporaries in the 1860s most likely would have self-identified as Creole. Not only was it the term in everyday use in their world, it was the official legal designation of their social caste, no small item in pre-Soviet Russia.

Dinneh is a variation of the word *Déné,* which in turn refers to the Native Alaskan people more commonly known today as Athabascans. (In Canada, Déné is the preferred term.) Northern Athabascan people, speaking a plethora of related languages, occupy the boreal forest across a vast swath of the northern part of North America; the western half of this range encompasses Alaska's Interior. The word *Athabascan*, it should be noted, is not their word. It is an Anglo corruption of a Cree place name—Lake Athabasca, in northern Alberta—and was first coined in 1836 by the armchair ethnographer Albert Gallatin.

In the 1860s, Athabascan people were nomadic, moving frequently around their country to find food. Often they carried nothing but their weapons, an axe, a kettle, and their bedding. Wives and mothers would have their sewing kits. Whatever technology they needed beyond that was made on the spot as needed from wood, leather, stone, or whatever else was at hand; as Lukin's Athabascan mother points out to him, camping gear is much easier to carry inside your head than on your back.

Early accounts from explorers along the lower Yukon River (or the Kwifpak, as the Russians knew it) often make note the ethnic differences between Athabascan people and the Yup'ik people of the coast and delta region. More often than not, the ethnonym they record is some version of *Dinneh.* Modern-day Athabascan people in Alaska divide themselves into thirteen different groups, each speaking a different language. Among these are the Tanana, Deghitan (formerly known as the Ingalik), Upper Kuskokwim, and the Koyukon. In Lukin's world, the latter two are known by the terms Koltsan and Denakeh, respectively.

Fort Kolmakov, also known as Kolmakovski, was a Russian America Company trading station on the middle Kuskokwim River, near the mouth of the Hohlitna River and the modern village of Sleetmute. It was established in 1833 by Fedor Kolmakov and Ivan Lukin's father, Semyon Lukin (both Alaska-born Creoles) after a series of explorations and trading trips to the Kuskokwim that started in 1816. Initially the station was just a small cluster of cabins, but in 1841 the operation was moved across the river and built into a more substantial facility. The location was a strategic point at the boundary between the Athabascan and Yup'ik worlds.

Semyon Lukin would spend the rest of his career with the Company managing this settlement and the fur commerce that flowed through it. His oldest son, Ivan Lukin, was tapped to succeed him; he probably seemed like the logical choice, having worked there with his father almost since the post's founding. But Ivan Lukin doesn't seem to have been, in modern parlance, management material. The Company relieved him from his duties for mismanagement and reassigned him to Saint Michael.

Fort Nulato was first established in 1839 by a Creole trader from Kenai named Malakov. His fort soon caught fire and burned to the ground. Vasili Deryabin rebuilt the post in 1842 and spent the next several years buying furs along the Kwifpak/Yukon River. At the same time, he searched constantly for the river's source. Deryabin was killed in 1851 when the Koyukuk River Athabascan chief known as Larion and several of his followers sacked and burned the fort. It was rebuilt soon after and continued to serve as the hub of Russian trade on the Kwifpak/Yukon River until the sale of the colony to the United States.

Ikogmiut Mission, known today in Alaska as Russian Mission, was the parish headquarters of the Russian Orthodox Church on the lower Kwifpak/Yukon. The name refers to the local Ikogmiut Yup'ik people. The Russian America Company also operated a trading station there, not the least because the settlement commanded the portage trail between the Yukon and Kuskokwim rivers. From Ikogmiut, a single Orthodox priest had to service a parish several hundred miles in circumference.

Kamelik was colonial Russian slang for a type of raincoat invented by the Unangan people of the Aleutian Islands. It was made from the small intestine of a sea lion that had been split and dried. This long strip of intestine would be sewn into a spiral shape that formed the body and sleeves of the garment, along with a hood. The finished product resembled a crinkly knee-length hoodie.

Originally the hem of the garment was made to be secured around the rim of a bidarka, which would then form a watertight barrier to keep water from pouring into the boat's hatch when paddling at sea.

Kolosh is the name the Russians applied to the Tlingit people of Southeast Alaska after their initial hostile encounters. Not surprisingly, the modern Tlingit don't care for the name, and never did, which is putting things mildly. The Tlingit of Lukin's day lived in large communal houses framed with large timbers and covered over with split cedar planks. Their villages were almost always by the seaside in sheltered harbors; food from the ocean and the forest was abundant in their country (and still is), which in turn supported a large, sedentary population, even by 19th century standards.

Kwifpak River was the name the Russians adopted for the Yukon River. Because their early explorations moved upstream from the coast, they naturally enough adopted the name used by the Yup'ik (or Yupiak, in an older spelling) people who lived around the delta and the lower river. The search for the source of the river became an obsession for a handful of Russian traders, chiefly Vasili Deryabin of Nulato. The British Hudson Bay Company, approaching from the east by way of the Porcupine River (also known as the Choonjik River), also chose a name used by the local people they encountered: Youcon, spelled today as Yukon.

Malimiut is a cultural division of the Yup'ik people of western Alaska. The Yup'ik in turn are one of the broad divisions of the people who used to be called Eskimos, along with the Inupiaq, Sugpiaq, and Chupik.

The Malimiut live around Norton Bay and the Saint Michael area. Other Yup'ik groups mentioned in this series include the Kitagmiut and Kuskowagmiut of the Kuskokwim River, and the Ikogmiut of the lower Yukon. Any name that ends in the suffix *-miut* denotes Yup'ik or Inupiaq people.

Nuklukayet (pronounced Noo-clew-ka-yet) lies at the mouth of the Tanana River where it joins the Yukon. For generations prior to the arrival of Europeans, Nuklukayet was a meeting place for all the Athabascan people of the middle Yukon drainage. It is often described in historical literature as a trade fair, but it was much more than that. After a long winter of hustling a living in the forest, people wanted to camp out on the beach, catch lots of salmon, and reunite with friends and family they hadn't seen since last year. Maybe even get an occasional nap while the grandparents watched their kids. Time at Nuklukayet was the closest thing these folks had in their lives to a summer holiday, though there was always the imperative to catch and dry enough salmon to last the winter.

Pitchka furnaces have a long and storied tradition in Russian culture, and this was brought over to Alaska. They were constructed of stone and mortar, usually in the center of a dwelling, and were engineered to retain heat through thermal mass. Some pitchkas were as big as a car. In former times they were as universal as modern oil or gas furnaces, but they also did double duty as the hearth and primary cooking appliance.

Russian America was the official name in the Russian Empire of the colony that would become Alaska. The Danish explorer Vitus Bering, sailing for the Russian government, is credited with discovering Alaska in 1741 (in much the same way that Columbus "discovered" the Americas). In his wake, private companies of Siberian fur hunters began crossing the Bering Sea looking for sea otters in the Aleutian Archipelago. Their pelts fetched astronomical sums in trade with China, and a man of limited means could quickly amass a fortune. They quickly figured out that it was much more efficient to force the local Unangan men to do the hunting, and to this end they established a pattern of kidnapping wives and children and holding them as "guests," and paying for the skins the husbands brought in with a knife, a kettle, or a handful of beads. This was paltry restitution by any measure.

More and more hunters kept making the crossing throughout the 1700s, and the enterprise became consolidated into the hands of a few competing companies. By the 1780s, the hunters from these companies were fighting with each other as much as with Native people. In response to this, Czar Paul I forced a merger of the two most prominent companies, the Shelhikov-Golikov Company and the Lebedev-Lastochkin Company. The new enterprise was known as the Russian America Company—RAC for short—and became the de facto government of the colony.

For much of the 1800s, the Russian Empire was locked in a bitter struggle with the British Empire; they were the two largest empires the world has ever seen. Russia pushed eastward across Asia and into the continental lobe of North America that we now call Alaska. The British, through their proxy the Hudson Bay Company, pushed north and west across the lakes and rivers of Canada. The two empires collided at the 141st meridian, fixed as the boundary line by an international treaty in 1829.

Saint Michael, also known as Mikhailovski, was both a trading station and the Russian administrative seat of the lower Kwifpak/Yukon River and Bering Sea coast. The posts of Nulato, Ikogmiut Mission, Unalakleet, and Andreivski all reported to the district manager at Saint Michael.

From Signals, Book Two of Seasons of Want and Plenty

They were sneaking back toward the camp when Lukin spotted the figure standing on the ice, watching them through the trees. The moon had risen sometime in the remnants of night, bigger than he had ever seen it, as if it had come closer to earth just to peer at him through the trees with the one eye not hidden by the shadow of the Earth.

"You go ahead," he said to Anfisa.

"What's wrong?"

"Nothing at all. But if anyone's awake it will look less suspect if we come to camp at different times from different directions."

She favored him with a sly look. "Sneaking around, are we?"

"We are both married."

Anfisa lifted his hand to her lips and kissed it. "The moon looks close tonight," she said, looking over his shoulder. Then she moved quietly through the spruce timber. Back at the slough the figure had moved to shore and was standing next to a cottonwood where the water swelled around its knobby roots. Lukin walked back down to the water.

"Hello, Zia."

"Happy springtime, Ivan."

"Yes. How was your winter?"

"Winter means nothing to me. I see you've found a new distraction."

"I think I might actually be in love with her."

She said nothing, watching him.

"You sent me a vision tonight."

"In your dreamworld. Yes."

"Why do you keep showing these things to me?"

"Because you want me to."

"Because you think it keeps me bound to you."

"Does it not?"

"What if I told you I no longer wish to see these things?"

Zia giggled and reached out to run a finger along his arm.

"There is a man with magic that can help you," Lukin said. "He lives up the River Tananah."

"Whatever you want, Ivan." Her mouth hooked up a little on one side, as if humoring a small child.

"What is this force that keeps you enslaved?"

"There is no force," she said. "I am the force."

"Zia, the time has come for this to end." In the moment it dawned on Lukin how tired he was of her and their conversations that seemed to go nowhere at all.

"You're tired of me?" She cocked her head at him. Somewhere up near the watching moon a thrush let out it's buzzing call, somewhere between a hum and a whistle. The iconography graven into its face and thrown into the relief of shadows suddenly had Lukin's blood up. Perhaps it was the dream of the Kolosh killing his grandmother, or perhaps he was just weary of never seeing the moon as it had been before he met Zia so long ago at the cove near New Archangel.

"I'm tired of trying to help you all these years and just going around in circles. A long time ago my father set free a slave girl. He spent part of his childhood enslaved by the Kolosh, and when he became a bidarshik he used to buy slaves whenever he could to free them."

"That slave girl grew up to be your wife."

Lukin sighed. "Yes. Yes, she did."

Zia bounced up onto her toes. "You want me to be your wife?"

"No."

She frowned at him.

"What I want is to do the right thing. That which God's law compels me to do."

"You know I don't like it when you say that." There came a thrumming feel through the world as she spoke, as if the moon itself was pulling the earth and everything upon it toward its open mouth. Lukin had only felt this once before, when Zia had tried to take him after Fort Youcon. It was like a wind, but far more viscous. The tree limbs swayed overhead. The open water of the pond began pushing toward the moon that now seemed even closer than before, bearing down upon him. Lukin's hair waved in the current like weeds in a stream.

"What are you doing?"

"You are not the only one who is tired of being played with, Ivan. You have a choice to make."

"You want my soul, not me. Don't pretend it's anything else."

She walked a circle around him. "You want to give your soul to the wife of that friend of yours. The one who caught us all those years ago back at the cove."

"Yosif Denisov," he said and realized too late the mistake he'd made. Now she knew his name. And that meant she had the opening she needed for him.

"Yosif Denisov," she said, turning the syllables over in her mouth. Lukin turned to keep facing her, or more specifically to avoid turning his back to her.

"You've already given your soul to her. I see it now, Ivan."

"I have given a piece of myself to her," Lukin said. "But it's a piece of my heart. My soul belongs to God and to my country."

"Yosif Denisov," she repeated, still scoring her circle. Her matted hair had grown more wild, and her teeth seemed longer, more fanglike. Without any warning she darted in at him and hissed, clacking her teeth together as she flashed a taunting smile that looked very much like the one the moon wore.

Lukin stood his ground. "This shaman on the Tananah has powerful magic. The most powerful I've ever encountered. We can set you free so that you no longer crave the souls of others." He was careful not to speak Tathyaldin's name.

"You will get rid of her," Zia said. Her voice sounded like the grinding of ice cakes in the spring breakup.

"Get rid of who?" His pulse hammered in his ears.

"Her. Denisov's wife." She glared at him from under her brows.

"I'm not going to do that."

Her eyes had turned solid black, the whites and irises gone as if they never were. "If you don't, I will kill him."

"That would be unwise, Zia."

"*I said get rid of her!*"

About the Author

Kris Farmen is a writer, editor, and historian. His books include *The Devil's Share*, *Turn Again*, *Edge of Somewhere*, and *Blue Ticket*. His work has also appeared in *Alaska* magazine, the *Anchorage Press*, and *Russian Life*, among others. He lives in Alaska with his wife, daughter, and rescue dog.

Read more at https://www.krisfarmen.com/.

www.ingramcontent.com/pod-product-compliance
Ingram Content Group UK Ltd.
Pitfield, Milton Keynes, MK11 3LW, UK
UKHW042003190726
13854UKWH00005B/2138

9 798215 151990